See What I See

GLORIA WHELAN

See What I See

HARPER TEEN
An Imprint of HarperCollinsPublishers

HarperTeen is an imprint of HarperCollins Publishers.

Library of Congress Cataloging-in-Publication Data
Whelan, Gloria.
    See what I see / Gloria Whelan. — 1st ed.
        p.   cm.
    Summary: When eighteen-year-old Kate arives on the Detroit
doorstep of her long-estranged father, a famous painter, she is
shocked to learn that he is dying and does not want to support
her efforts to attend the local art school.
    ISBN 978-0-06-125545-8
    [1. Fathers and daughters—Fiction. 2. Artists—Fiction.
3. Sick—Fiction. 4. Duty—Fiction. 5. Detroit (Mich.)—Fiction.]
I. Title.
PZ7.W5718Sf 2011   2010003094
[Fic]—dc22   CIP
                                                          AC

Typography by Alison Klapthor
11 12 13 14 15   LP/RRDB   10 9 8 7 6 5 4 3 2 1
❖
First Edition

For Paula Coppedge

1

I see my life in paintings. Right now I see my mom as a painting by the artist de Kooning, a scribbled woman, all angry eyes and open mouth with sharp teeth. We're both standing in the kitchen of our trailer, which means we're inches from each other. "Don't do this!" she shouts at me. "I've spent the last twelve years of my life protecting you from that man."

She's talking about my dad, her emotions bubbling over with a combination of hatred for him, fear for me, and anger with herself for not having the money to send me to art school. I understand, but I'm going to go anyhow. "He's not 'that man,'" I say. "He's my father, and staying with him is the only way I can go to art school. I'm going to school so I can come back. Honestly, Mom, you know everything I want to paint is right here." I look out the small trailer window at the line of birch trees. A few of the leaves have already turned yellow. Bronze yellow, I decide, with a touch of brilliant yellow green. I match everything against my chart of acrylic paints.

"Your father hasn't had anything to do with you since you were a child. I don't care what optimistic story you've invented about him; the last thing he'll want is his daughter moving in with him, interfering with his work and spoiling his latest romance."

I know Mom is right. Last spring, as soon as I was accepted, I wrote to my father in Detroit, begging him to let me move in with him while I go to school. I told him that not only had I been accepted at the school, but after they saw my work, I'd been promised a scholarship too. "I don't need money from you," I wrote Dad. "I certainly don't want to cash in on your fame.

I just need a place to stay." In my letter I told him that I knew how important his work was and I swore I wouldn't get in his way. I even offered to clean his house and cook for him. He never answered that letter, or the others I sent, in spite of the fact that I've led my mother to think he agreed to my coming. I'm just going to knock on his door. I can't believe he'll turn me away. It's amazing what you can talk yourself into.

If I'm going to be an artist, I need to get to know my dad. He's a famous painter; I want to know his secrets; I want to learn from him . . . but there is something else. He's my *father*. After all these years of being curious about him, why wouldn't I want a chance to know him?

Because of how Mom feels about Dad, right after the divorce Mom changed my name to her maiden name. I'm Kate Tapert, not Kate Quinn, daughter of the famous Dalton Quinn. I don't blame Mom. She and Dad grew up here in this northern Michigan town of Larch that's so little it isn't even on a lot of maps. They married right out of high school. Mom has thrown out all the photographs that have Dad in them, but years ago I went to the library and looked through old issues of the *Larch Chronicle* until I found the account of their wedding. Wedding pictures are full of promise. Mom was looking at Dad as if he was a movie star, and Dad was staring down at her with a foolish grin like a kid with a new puppy. They were eighteen, the same age I am now. Bad things shouldn't happen to people that age.

After they got married, they moved into a small frame house right on Maple Street. I see it whenever I go to town. They left that house a long time ago, and for a lot of years it was run-down and empty, but a young couple bought it last year, fixed it all up, and put a swing on the front porch. Sometimes now, when I walk by the house, I pretend that I'm just a kid again and that Mom and Dad live there and that they're happy.

When they were newlyweds, Dad worked for his father's construction business. Some days he wouldn't turn up. He'd stay home painting instead. Soon he began to sell his work in the galleries of the nearby tourist towns of Traverse City and Petoskey. His dad didn't approve of his painting, and when the construction company got in trouble because Dad played hooky too often, causing the company to fall behind on a job, Granddad and Dad had a big argument and Dad got fired.

That's when my parents headed for Detroit. Mom worked in downscale restaurants that smelled like grease and served coffee in chipped cups. Dad painted. I've heard often enough from Mom what that was like. Mom smiled hard all day at creeps to get tips so she and Dad could scrape by, and Dad painted all day and drank all night. And there were other women. Dad was furious when I came along and began to interfere with his work.

I've blocked out a lot of memories of those days in Detroit. The three of us were like a series of paintings by the Dutch artist Karel Appel. The paintings are of two adults and a child, and in each one the three figures become more and more distorted, more chaotic. When I first saw the series, it grabbed me and I know why. That was our world. It was mostly arguments. The words I had to listen to were so cruel, I didn't want anything to do with words. I stopped talking when I was five, and Mom had to take me to a psychologist. In her office the psychologist had a large dollhouse with tiny lamps that actually lit up and little dishes for the tables. At first I loved to play with it, but as I moved the dolls around, she would ask questions like "Why is the mama doll angry?" or "Why isn't the papa doll home?" That spoiled the dollhouse for me, and I wouldn't answer her.

There are good memories, too. Mom found a restaurant where the owner felt sorry for her and let her bring me to work, so I wouldn't get in Dad's way. I'd sit on a tall stool in the restaurant kitchen chewing on raw carrots and watching Ed, the short-order cook, flip burgers and put the potatoes in the fryer. The potatoes came out a rich shade of gold. When Mom's back was turned, Ed sneaked me some. I can still remember the taste of the salt and the crisp and soft of each bite.

I remember Dad as a force of nature, like a wind that comes without warning, rattling windows and bending trees. His voice was loud, as if he dared you not to listen. Watching him work was how I got interested in painting. If Mom didn't take me to work, Dad would give me a scrap of canvas and a brush and some paint to keep me occupied. It made Mom crazy, because the paint would get all over my hair and clothes. Even after all these years the smell of paint brings back the image of my father, like some genie escaping from a lamp—an evil genie, Mom would say.

When a gallery in New York City sold one of Dad's paintings, he took the money and followed the painting east, leaving us behind. Mom and I came back here to Larch, and Mom kept waitressing. Her uniform this time was dark green with a white apron that she had to wash and iron every night, no matter how late she got home from work, because she had only the one.

Dad never wrote; he never sent money. People told Mom to get a court order for child support, but she was too proud. Dad came back to Larch just one more time, when his mother—my grandmother—died. I was nine. I hadn't seen Dad in years, but because he was famous I had seen pictures of him in newspapers and magazines, had, in fact, searched for those pictures. He was a big-shouldered man, tall with sandy hair and a fierce, impatient look. *Why are you wasting my time?* he seemed to be demanding of the photographers.

Dad had arrived at the church for his mother's funeral wearing jeans and cowboy boots, as if he had come from Montana instead of New York City. His hair was long, curling around his shoulders. He didn't look like anyone else in Larch, and he certainly didn't look like he was at a funeral.

It made Mom so angry just to be in the same room with him that her hands were clenched. I betrayed Mom by edging away from her a little, thinking if I did, he might come over to me. He didn't, but I caught him looking hard at me as if I were some new plant or animal life. He didn't stay for the church lunch but hurried away immediately after the funeral.

A couple of weeks later I received an elaborate French doll. It came with a fancy silk dress and a coat trimmed in real fur. Letting me keep the doll must have been one of the hardest things Mom ever had to do. I wrote a long thank-you note right away, telling Dad all about me and what I was doing at school, what books I was reading, and what treasures I had found in the woods. I struggled to write it in cursive and copied it over twice before I was satisfied. I even drew a little picture of pine trees and enclosed it in the letter, wanting to show my father I was an artist too. Seeing him again that day in church made me want to be an artist, because it would finally give me some connection to my father. He never wrote back.

My first big argument with Mom came when I spent my babysitting money on a paint set. She almost threw it out. I couldn't blame her. Here I was reaching for the very thing that had more or less ruined her life. It was as if my dad had been a murderer and I had gone out and bought a gun.

Then last year I saw a short article in a Detroit

newspaper saying Dalton Quinn had moved from New York back to Detroit, was broke and living in an old house, and had become a recluse. He even refused an interview with the reporter who covered the Detroit art scene. The article listed Dad's awards and said, "Dalton Quinn was once considered one of America's most well-known artists, but after a fast lifestyle, and then rumors that he was no longer painting, he dropped out of sight." The article mentioned the street he lived on, and there was a picture of his house with the number above the door.

Mom saw the article too. She was suspicious and nervous about Dad's moving to Detroit. Although he was two hundred miles away, he was in the same state. After a couple of months went by and we heard nothing from him, Mom began to relax.

Then I applied to the Detroit art school, and now I'm planning to move in with my father. Naturally she hates the idea. Our trailer is filled with trip wires and land mines. There are explosions all day long. Mom even accused me of wanting to go to the school just so

I can be with Dad. But I'm going because painting is my life. How can I make her see that? I don't know.

Our arguments end like they always do—with us crying and hugging each other because we're all we have. Plus we live six miles from town in a trailer. It's close quarters, and there's not much room to sulk. So we cry a little and make up.

Our trailer is planted on an acre of cutover land. All around us are miles of woods. The woods are like a house, and I wander from room to room. There is the birch-tree room with acres of white trunks slashing across green mosses. There is the pond room with its family of beavers. There is the swamp room with cedar and larch trees growing out of black water and the feeling that some hidden thing is watching you. The woods are the house I truly live in. And they were where I headed as soon as the school bus dropped me off in the afternoons. When I first started painting, they were what I painted: the white birches, the black water, the reflection of a giant pine in the pond.

One Christmas I begged for snowshoes so I could

visit the woods in winter. The snowshoes let me see the hares, brown in the summertime, white against the snow. I discovered how you could paint white on white, and the dozens of different shades of white. I invented a whole new vocabulary of whites, from sun white to shadow white.

I head to the woods now, but I carry my argument with my mother with me like a heavy stone. Honestly, I'm not sure about art school. The school said I have talent and I can't imagine doing anything but painting. It's what I want, but I still don't know if I'm doing the right thing. Is it worth making Mom so unhappy? Am I being selfish just like Dad was, thinking only of myself?

My boyfriend, Justin, has been encouraging me. He's in my class at school and I've been dating him forever, but a lot of that is habit and friendship, not something serious. He's a technology geek, and when I told him about the art school, he helped me make a DVD of my paintings to send with my application. The school asked me down last spring for an interview. I told Mom I was going on an all-day picnic to the sand dunes near Traverse City with Justin, and he drove me the four hours down to Detroit. I shriveled when I saw how large Detroit was. Nothing was familiar. The city was crammed with buildings, and even Justin was intimidated by the way cars rushed past us on the expressways as if speed limits had never been invented.

The art school was designed by a famous architect and put together like steel Tinkertoys, with lots of glass and a terrific sculpture garden right in the middle of it. Just across the street is Detroit's art museum. All these things were so close, I could wrap my arms around them.

The school had its own gallery hung with the work of students. As I admired the drawings and paintings, I imagined my own work there. I looked into the empty classrooms and saw the paint-stained easels. Everything seemed *right*. A woman, "Call Me Terry," interviewed me. Why had I chosen that school? I had asked for a scholarship; what was my financial situation? How long had I been painting? What did I plan to do after

I graduated? Did I understand the school was a college and I would be required to take some academic courses, that it wouldn't be just art? I gave routine answers. Then she asked, "Is your interest in art a kind of hobby?"

"Not a hobby," I said, and without thinking I rattled on about how it was only when I was painting that I was really alive, how I didn't ever want to do anything else, how I wanted to show everyone that you could paint a single leaf a hundred different ways, depending on the season and the light and how you felt about the leaf right at that moment, and I loved that sometimes when you're painting, you surprise yourself by what appears on the canvas. When I finally stopped talking, she told me how much she had liked the work I had sent and how my view of nature was unique—*unique* was the actual word she used. When she promised me the scholarship, I knew nothing would stop me. I ran out to the car, where Justin was waiting, and threw my arms around him. I didn't want to leave the school. I wanted to pitch a tent right there in the middle of the sculpture garden.

The ride back on I-75 took four hours, and in all that time I wasn't able to figure out how to tell Mom. A couple of weeks before my birthday, when Mom asked me what I wanted, I finally got the courage to say I didn't want a gift—what I wanted more than anything was to go to art school. I told her about the interview and the scholarship and how they liked my work. She was furious, and there was a week of angry silence alternating with the banging of pots and pans. Over the summer Mom almost got used to the idea, but now my insisting on staying with Dad had started our arguments all over again.

I have the woods to myself this afternoon as usual. Alone in the woods I stop thinking about the argument and lose myself in looking. I consider a gray football-shaped hornets' nest in the top of a beech tree. The hornets are still flying in and out, but I can imagine the hornets' nest in the rain and snow, peeling away layer by layer, exposing the thousands of little papery cells. In the middle of the pond the beavers have added more branches to their lodge. I see the haphazard way the branches are woven together. Then I discover a castle of moss, the decayed stump of a pine tree covered with humps of bright green moss and shreds of grayish green lichen. Stretched out beside the stump is a pencil-thin green snake. I stare and stare, memorizing the bright green of the snake and the yellow green of the moss and the gray green of the lichen and the snake's little black eye. I hurry home and get out my paints.

2

*M*om stands at the door, wiping away her tears with the back of her hand. I know they're genuine. Mom never uses tears as a weapon. If I didn't have my suitcase to hang on to and the weight of my backpack pushing me ahead, I'd give up right there and then.

In a tight voice Mom says, "Call me as soon as you get to the city." The restaurant bought her a cell phone so they could get hold of her if something came up and she was needed. Now she put me on her account and gave me my own phone, as if I'm heading for a combat zone and might need backup—and maybe I will.

As I ride with Justin, I can't stop thinking of how Mom looked when I said good-bye to her. With the dark woods lurking behind our house and Mom standing all alone on the porch with a single shaft of morning light falling on her, it was just like a Vermeer painting.

Justin takes me to the bus stop. Mom thinks he's going to drive me all the way to Detroit, but I won't let him. If Dad kicks me out, I don't want Justin to see it happen. He has no idea who my dad is, and if for some reason I have to come back home, I can just make up a story about Dad having to move away for his job.

"We're lucky to be getting away from this place," Justin says. Unlike me, Justin plans to head for a big city when he's finished with school. He wants to work his way up to the top of something. In addition to being a techie, he's a math genius. Even now, 50 percent of his attention is on me and my plight and 50 percent is on adding up the bus schedule posted on the blackboard over the counter, as if the schedule were a column of figures. Everything Justin owns, and sometimes the backs of his hands and the steam on his car windows, is covered with math problems. If you go shopping with him at a grocery store, he has the exact change out before the clerk even starts to add everything up. He has a scholarship for an engineering school in Michigan's Upper Peninsula. I envy him the nearness of Lake Superior and the miles of woods while I'm going to have to survive living in a city, away from all the things I love to paint. "Send me leaves," I tell him, "and twigs and feathers."

Justin's growing a beard for school, and his goodbye kiss is prickly, like our relationship. I like Justin, but lately I've had the feeling he considers me just another problem to work out, and once he does he'll lose interest. We're going in different directions. He wants to get away from Larch and I want to come back.

Some of the passengers on the bus settle down comfortably with copies of *Time* and *People* and bags of

M&M's, not caring where they are. Others treat their bus windows like TV screens with no remotes, staring hopefully at everything. A couple of young kids across the aisle have a sullen, spooked look as if they've been hijacked. I wonder if they're on a visit to see a divorced parent. I want to tell them they're lucky if they get to see both their mom and their dad, even if it's separately.

I force myself to sit quietly in my seat as everything familiar disappears. I have qualms and wonder what a qualm would look like if you painted it—probably like a bowl of melting ice cream or a dish of Jell-O just before it sets.

I panic a little as I watch the countryside's empty fields and its acres of trees turn into small towns and then bigger towns. The trip takes hours, but it's much too fast. I don't want the moment to come when I have to face my father, but almost before I know it, there is Detroit itself. It seems to me there are many Detroits. First there are the suburbs with large houses and green lawns, but when the bus approaches downtown, I see deserted streets and boarded-up stores and vacant lots like a mouth of pulled teeth where houses once were. It's a city like an Edward Hopper painting with an emptiness that worries you, as if all the people were lost and no one was looking for them. Then suddenly everything comes alive again. There are glitzy restaurants, tangles of expressways, and stunning new sports stadiums. At the baseball stadium's entrance there are two gigantic tigers with welcoming, loopy grins.

I unfold my numb body and stumble out of the bus and into the station, where people sit in long sleepy rows looking dazed, as if they've been airlifted there and then abandoned. Back home I studied a map of Detroit, so I know Dad's street isn't too far from downtown. It's the section of Detroit where I lived with Mom and Dad. I wander outside and smell the city smell that is part cars, part french fries, and part wind kicking up dirt. A taxi driver and I exchange wordless looks. Mine says, *How about it?* his, *Hop in.* When I give the address, the driver says in a regretful voice, "Not far." He isn't going to get much money. I look at his license posted on the back of the front seat. There is his picture with a big smile, as if he's been waiting all his life to drive taxis. Maybe he has. His first name is Fikry. His last name has consonants and vowels in a strange order I can't pronounce.

"You coming home from a trip, or what?" Fikry asks.

"No. I'm going to stay with my dad for a while, but he doesn't know I'm coming." I don't know why I say that, except it's so heavy on my mind, it just slips out.

"What are you? Some kind of surprise?"

"No. He knows all about me."

"Your mother kick you out?"

"No. It's my idea. I'm going to art school here in Detroit."

"Where you from?"

"Northern Michigan."

"Snow all the time up there."

I see blocks of small, well-kept houses that appear to be a couple of hundred years old. The houses are huddled together, looking as if they need protection from all the craziness of the city. Each home has its square of perfect lawn. There are hanging baskets of petunias and pots of geraniums in an alizarin crimson hue. Many of the yards have tiny, immaculate rose gardens. Along the sidewalks run borders of sweet alyssum and beds of daisies and marigolds in bright copper and light cadmium yellow light hues.

"This is the street."

After the tall busyness of the commercial buildings downtown, here is this village right in the middle of the city. I am amazed. Nothing is familiar. There are churches and small stores with signs in languages I don't understand. I ask Fikry.

"Some Polish, some Albanian and Chaldean. Here's the house," he says. "You want me to wait and see how the surprise goes?"

"No, thanks."

Fikry coasts slowly to the end of the block and stops. Curious? Caring? I give him the benefit of the doubt.

Dad's place looks like the rest of the little houses, except his grass hasn't been cut and the only landscaping is a medley of weeds and a couple of empty cans. What is he doing here?

I drag my suitcase up the porch stairs. At the end of the block Fikry finally drives away. I miss him already. I stand there for a long minute, considering whether the smart thing would be to get on a bus and go back to Mom. No. Not yet. I push the doorbell, and when there is no answer, I knock. Nothing. Dad might have seen me and isn't answering on purpose, or he could be lost in his painting and not hear me. Heck, he could have gone back to New York. I try looking in the windows, but the shades are drawn. I knock at the back door. Nothing. I try the front doorbell again. I imagine how I look standing on the porch with my suitcase beside me. Pathetic.

At last the door jerks open. The hair that hangs around my father's shoulders is now thinner and grizzled with gray. His cheeks have sunk, and his skin is the faded yellow of old newspaper. His clothes are a size too large, or his body is a size too small. The hand on the door is scrawny and blue with veins. His voice is weak but furious, and his eyes are like two black weapons as he stares at me. "If you're a reporter, you can get the hell out of here or I'll have the police on you for trespassing."

I can barely get out "It's me, Dad. Kate."

He peers at me as if I'm something that has stuck to his shoe. "What do you think you're doing here? How did you find me? This is no time for a family reunion. I'm getting ready for a show and I need to be left alone."

"You're still painting? You look like you're sick."

"My health is not your concern, and yes, I'm painting. But I certainly wouldn't be able to work with a child running around the house. I suppose your mother sent you to spy on me. Well, you can turn around and go back to wherever you came from, and you are certainly not to suggest to your mother or anyone else that I'm ill."

"I'm not a child, and Mom has nothing to do with my being here. She's furious with me for coming. I told you in my letters that I have a scholarship at the art school, but I don't have money for housing. All I want is a place to sleep. I promise I won't get in your way, and if you aren't well, I can do things for you."

"I don't need anyone to do things for me, certainly not some amateur artist who's deluded into thinking she can paint."

Desperate, I plead, "Could I at least spend the night before I go back? I've traveled a couple of hundred miles on a bus to get here." I blink fast to fight off the tears. I thought I was prepared to be sent away, but maybe you can never be prepared for that.

Still hanging on to the door for support, he steps aside, regarding me as if I am an alien crashing into his space.

I hurry into the house with my suitcase and slip out of my backpack. Possession is nine-tenths of the law. I leave my things in the hall and follow my dad into the kitchen, which looks more like the last day of a garage sale than a place where you actually sit down to eat. Dirty dishes cover the counters; magazines and books are piled on the table and chairs. Unaccountably, a lawn mower is parked in one corner. A laptop computer is propped up on the stove top, its screen saver a shot of New York City's Grand Central Station in the thirties.

Dad sinks down on a chair after first removing a pile of soiled clothes. "Coffee's on the shelf."

I find the coffee hanging out with a couple of cans of baked beans and a bigger variety of Campbell's soups than you'd find in a grocery store. I empty the coffeemaker of what must have been the morning's brew and rinse it out.

Dad says, "I like it strong."

"So do I."

We watch in loud silence as the coffee drips, as if the slow trickle is the most interesting thing we have ever seen. I pour two cups, taking pains to get the same amount into each cup as if it's a test I'm taking, and hand one to Dad.

He brings the cup up to his mouth with a shaking hand and swallows so slowly, I imagine the coffee making its way around a complicated maze in his throat. There are no questions like *How is your mom?* or *What have you been doing since I last saw you ten years ago?*

No problem. I'm willing to go more than half-way. "My favorite painting of yours is the one in the Whitney Museum, the one of the woman in the red dress." Most of the figures in my father's portraits look like the people have begun to melt, morphing into splotches of color. Even the portraits you might recognize as people are like reflections in a fun-house mirror, distorted and grotesque. In all their ugliness, they're powerful, although you do have to wonder what goes on in his head. But there's something attractive about the woman in the red dress. That's why it's my favorite.

"The woman in red is Julia, someone I particularly dislike."

"But not when you painted her."

"No, not when I painted her." When he has emptied his cup, he puts it down and begins to work his way out of his chair. When I move to help him, he slaps my hand away. "I don't need your help."

"Dad, what's wrong with you?"

"Nothing."

"Right. Will you show me what you're working on now?"

"Certainly not." He indicates the computer. "You can get tomorrow's bus schedule online. There's a vacant room upstairs." He looks at my suitcase as if it contains something dangerous, a bomb or an eviction notice. "No need to unpack that." He disappears into what must be the living room. Before he slams the door shut, I have a glimpse of paintings stacked against a wall, their vivid colors like shouts. So that's his studio. One more part of his life I'm shut out of.

I tiptoe past Dad's studio, listening to the grunts and curses and happy shouts. It sounds like he's engaged in ferocious warfare and enjoying it. Upstairs I find the empty bedroom. The walls are a dark, depressing green, the color of a rain poncho, and on the ceiling is a water stain that looks a little like an abstract painting. There's an iron bed and a dresser with one drawer missing. A small shag rug lies on the wood floor like a sleeping dog. Ugly as the room is, I'd give anything to stay here. In the trailer I've never had a room of my own, just a pull-down bed where I can't curl up during the day.

I peek into Dad's room. I know he'd hate my poking around in his space, but I'm just catching up. After all these years I'm desperate to know something about the man who is my father. Dad's bed is a squirrel's nest of soiled sheets, looking like they need vacuuming more than changing. His clothes are draped over a chair, and books are piled up next to the bed. I'm about to back out of the room when I see it tucked into the edge of his mirror. It's wrinkled and a chunk of sky is missing, but it's the drawing of a pine tree I sent Dad all those years ago. I edge nearer to the dresser to get a better look, feeling like someone has just swept their hand over me, erasing everything I had believed about Dad's feelings for me. I *have* been a part of his life, even if I was nothing more than a piece of paper stuck in a mirror. When I didn't even know it, he was thinking of me. That does it. I won't give up. I'll find a way to stay. I don't care what it takes.

After a long minute of staring at the picture, my watery eyes drop to an official-looking letter on the top of the dresser. It's addressed to Dad and comes from some sort of medical department. A committee is informing Dad that regretfully they cannot recommend a liver transplant for him. They commend him for having "abstained from alcohol as is required for a transplant," and they're sure that will be "beneficial to his advanced cirrhosis," but his physical examination indicates "a dilated congestive cardiomyopathy," which eliminates him from consideration for a transplant. They say they are "sorry."

I hurry downstairs, pausing at the door to Dad's studio to be sure he's still painting. The sounds of work are there. I go online and Google "advanced cirrhosis" and "dilated congestive cardiomyopathy." I learn that without a liver transplant, which he isn't going to get, Dad's liver is giving out. And his heart isn't that strong either. He's dying. And he's alone.

Suddenly it's not all about me. Art school is

important, but there's another reason for me to be here. Dad needs me. It takes a long minute for that to sink in, and then I make my decision and hatch my desperate plan. I know what I'm going to do and I know Dad will be furious, but I don't care. He can't send me away because I won't go. Whatever he says.

When I open the door to his studio, he swings around, fuming. "You have no business interrupting me. This is exactly what I was afraid of. Now get out."

His paintings are gathered around him like children. There are a half dozen, many unfinished. Looking back at me from the easel and leaning against the wall are portraits. Dad has managed to discover ugliness in nearly every one of the people he paints. If they're fat, the fat hangs in ghastly folds, the faces puffed and bloated. If they're old, their sagging skin is a purplish white, their elbows and knees sharp angles, and their toenails curling and yellow. Children have blank, cruel faces, as if they're plotting evil mischief. I know these devastating portraits are amazing. I know they made Dad famous. But I hate them for what they do to people. What is he trying to say with them?

I'm not sure where I get the courage to follow through on my plan. It's more than my need to paint and my longing for art school. It's more than wanting to get close to Dad, to know him after all these years. It's even more than seeing my picture stuck in his mirror. Dad needs me because he doesn't have anyone else. I plunge in. "I read the letter from the doctors about your not getting a transplant. Even if you won't admit it, you have to have someone to take care of you. Let me stay. It's not just me feeling sorry for you. I'll get to go to school. It's an even trade."

He shouts, "What do you mean sneaking around and prying into my affairs? I should never have let you into this house. You can get out right now. Sleep on the street, for all I care. I don't need you and I don't want you here."

It's now or never. I take a breath. "If you don't let me stay, I'll tell Mom and the newspapers and your gallery how sick you are. You won't have your show."

He grabs a tube of paint and flings it at me. It isn't

even a near miss. His laughter comes out choked, as if it got strangled in his throat. He sinks into a chair and puts his hands over his face. When he takes his hands away, his face looks naked and I see more than he wants me to. Then he grins at me as if he's discovered some wicked secret too good not to share. "No question you're my daughter. Here's the bargain. I'm not driving anymore. You do the shopping, get me to the doctor, prepare my food, and answer my emails. You keep out of the way. I don't want to see more of you than I have to. You'll speak only when spoken to, and you can get out of my sight right now."

"Fine," I say. "It's a deal." I slam the door behind me and scurry back to my room. I have what I want, but what else do I have? I'm letting myself be locked in with a man who's going to die, a man I don't much like and who doesn't like me at all, a man who hates having me here.

I hear Lucinda Williams singing "Are You Alright?" on my cell ring. It's Mom's favorite song. "So are you all right?" Mom asks when I pick it up.

"Sure," I say. "I'm all settled in and everything's fine." I gulp down a sob. "I miss you." I try to picture Mom sitting in what we call the cozy corner of the trailer, where there's a bench with soft cushions and a lamp. It's where we curl up to read or watch our favorite TV shows. I hate thinking of Mom there alone.

"What's his house like?" Mom asks.

She won't say his name. "It's fine. I have a nice room," I reassure her. "Dad's busy painting, so I won't see much of him. Once I start school next week, I'll be gone most of the time."

"You promise to come home if things don't work out? I mean if he gets to be too much."

"Yes," I tell her, "I promise."

What is too much? I ask myself.

3

On this first night in Dad's house I have trouble sleeping. I go over and over what I have done. I've promised to take care of Dad, but I might as well have promised to care for an injured lion that might turn on me at any minute. Still, I tell myself, it was the right thing to do. At one point I hear Dad tramping down the stairs, followed by the sound of his studio door opening and closing. I want to see if he's all right, but something tells me he wouldn't be happy to have me checking on him. After all these years I have my father back and he's going to die. It's unfair. Then I think of my father locked into his studio downstairs and what it must be like for him to think of all the pictures he will never get to paint.

I give up on sleeping, and by dawn I'm downstairs. Dad is moving around in the studio, talking to himself. When I knock on the door and offer him coffee, he looks at me as if he has no idea who I am. But he takes the coffee. I'm surprised at how happy that makes me.

"Do you want a fried egg or something?" I offer.

"A fried egg?" He makes it sound like something exotic, something no one in his right mind would think of eating. The door slams shut. Taking care of him is going to be harder than I thought.

I decide I can at least do something about the mess in the kitchen. Growing up in a trailer, I learned early on that neatness is everything; otherwise, with so little room, you get buried under piles of stuff. I do all the dirty dishes that have been dumped in the sink. I stack the avalanche of art books and magazines. I empty the fridge of everything that looks older than I am, leaving the shelves nearly bare. Maybe when he sees I'm willing to be helpful, Dad will put up with me a little better.

A phone rings. There must be an extension in the studio, so I wait a minute to see if Dad's going to answer. He doesn't. Whoever it is won't give up. I pick up the receiver. "Hello?" There's dead silence and then a woman's angry voice. "Who are you? Where's Dalton?"

"I'm Dalton's daughter, and he's in his studio painting."

"If you're his daughter, I'm the Mona Lisa. He certainly never mentioned a daughter. Whoever you are, I feel sorry for you. You may as well know, if you don't already, living with Dalton is hell. Just tell him Julia called. He knows where to reach me."

The woman in red. She looked so nice in the painting. Did she change? Was it something Dad did that made her change? Will staying with him change me? The phone rings again. Thinking it's the same woman, I pick it up and hiss, "Yes?"

A man's voice. "Who are you? Where's Dalton?"

The questions of the day. This time I say, "I'm Kate Tapert. Dalton is in his studio."

"Just where he should be. I'm delighted to hear your voice. Dalton always works at his best when he has a muse to inspire him. Just keep an eye on the bottle, will you? You probably know his tendencies."

Indignant I say, "I'm his daughter, and Dad's not drinking."

"Well, two surprises. I hope you aren't creating complications. In my experience children tend to be distracting. How is your father, by the way? Behaving himself?"

"He's fine. Who is this?"

"Sorry, I should have told you. I'm Ian Morgan. I have a little gallery in New York. Your father is having a show here in January. I don't think it would be immodest of me to say it will be the culmination of his life's work. Not that he doesn't have many years ahead of him, of course, but it will be a kind of summing up, and the advance publicity has been even beyond my expectations. However, to have a show, one must have paintings, and so far your father's shipments have been sparse. When am I going to see his new work?"

Ian Morgan. Everyone who has anything to do with the art world knows the Morgan Gallery. It's the most famous contemporary-art gallery in New York. Excited, I say, "Soon, and they're wonderful. The best things he's done." The least I can do is talk Dad's work up. "Do you want to speak with my father?"

"No, indeed. Not if he's working. I trust you understand the importance of the show and that you won't be bothering him."

"No. I'm just here to sort of look after the house."

"How nice. You'll stay out of the way of the studio? No dusting or scrubbing his canvases?" There was a mirthless laugh at his little joke. "Tell him I'm impatient to see what he's doing." He hangs up.

Dad emerges. "Who was that?" he demands.

"It was Ian Morgan. He wants to know when he'll have more paintings. I told him soon."

"Did you? I'm afraid you're something of an optimist."

"You must be excited about having an exhibition at the Morgan Gallery. Any artist would die for the privilege of showing there." I catch myself. *Die.* It just slipped out.

"Yes, well, it may come to that."

Hastily I change the subject. "A woman named Julia called."

"Ah, the woman in red. A veritable virago. You can take all my calls after this. I don't want to talk with anyone. Just explain I'm working."

"Dad, why did you come back to Detroit? Was it because you don't want anyone in New York to know you're sick?"

He stares at me for a minute, and I wonder if he's asking himself whether talking with me is a total waste of time. One more thing to keep him from his painting. He sighs. "That was part of it. And a little superstition. The paintings that gave me my start were done in this city, and rental houses here are a lot cheaper than a studio apartment in New York." He shoots me an alligator grin. "That's enough. You're as bad as a reporter." He glances at the newly cleaned kitchen but doesn't say anything.

"What can I do for you?" I ask.

"I suppose you can put a dinner together?"

"Now that I've cleaned out the mold, there's nothing in the fridge."

He reaches into his wallet, extracts a couple of bills, and tosses them at me. "There's a convenience store at the end of the street run by a Chaldean family."

"What's Chaldean?"

"Middle Eastern and connected to the Catholic church, one of those peoples who are chased from country to country."

I close the door of the house behind me, scaring off a feral cat. Its fur is mangy, and one ear has been bitten off. It stops and snarls at me. Even the cat wants me gone. Now that I'm free, maybe I should just keep walking and not return. I worry that the house is a huge vacuum sucking me into Dad's world and away from my own. The woman in red said, "Living with Dalton is hell." Maybe I ought to take that as a warning. I wonder if I will be able to care for Dad if he becomes really ill and how much time that will take. But then I tell myself to stop whining. None of this matters. The important thing is that school starts next week.

I'm relieved to be outdoors, but it's not the out-of-doors I'm used to. The sun looks tired, as if it's worked its way through layers and layers of city to get here, and when I take a deep breath, it seems like I'm inhaling what a thousand automobiles have just exhaled. As I walk along the city streets, I look at the houses, shut up tight. Where are all the people?

There's nothing around to cheer me up. Even the leaves on the trees seem dusty. A few English sparrows fly up from the sidewalk. I'm homesick for woods and uncommon birds, and I worry that all I'll be able to paint here in the city are my memories of up north.

When I come to it, the store is a surprise. The outside is painted burnt sienna with a cheerful slash of French ultramarine blue. Inside you can barely move without running into displays of cereal boxes and water bottles. There are flyers tacked to the walls advertising Polish festivals, Albanian meetings, and a Chaldean church service.

"What can I do for you?" The man behind the counter has white hair, dark brown eyes, and a fan of wrinkles around his eyes. Though it's warm out, he's wearing an old wool cardigan. "Have I seen you before?" he asks.

"No. I just got here. I'm staying with my dad, who lives down the block. Mr. Quinn?"

"I'm Emmanuel, and I know your father. Sometimes when I don't see him for a few days, I send my boy with a little food for him. It's good you came to watch over him. There's too much of families falling apart. That's not right."

"Well, the falling apart in our family was his idea."

"I don't say right or wrong. I only say when you're old it's hard to get on by yourself. I've got four kids and they've all worked right here in the store." He points to a boy about ten, who is piling up cookie boxes. "Joseph here gives me a hand after school." Joseph grins and goes on piling one box on top of another as if it's a game you keep playing until you reach the point when all the boxes tumble down. I imagine what it would be like to grow up in a grocery store with food always there like wrapped gifts just for the taking, only of course you wouldn't take them.

"Your father never gets anything fresh. Just stuff out of cans. That's why he's not looking so good. What he needs are fresh fruits and vegetables. Look at these tomatoes I just got in. They're right from the Eastern Market. The farmer was unloading them from his truck just this morning. And how about a little fresh poultry? This chicken is only a day from the hen-house. You wait a minute and I'll cut it up for you."

A guy a little older than me wanders in, holding a book. He has a pencil stuck behind his ear. He's tall, with Emmanuel's dark brown eyes. "Put your book down for a minute, Thomas, and give me a hand with this chicken. You're the expert on cutting up."

Thomas lays his hand on the chicken almost tenderly and reaches for a cruel knife. He studies the chicken like it's a final exam, then gives me a killer grin.

"My son is showing off for a pretty girl. He's in medical school and one day he's going to be a surgeon." To Thomas he says, "This is Mr. Quinn's girl." And to me, "What's your name?"

"Kate."

Thomas neatly dismembers the chicken. "This boy studies all the time," Emmanuel says. He gives his son an approving look. "He already knows from his books what's going on inside of us. What do you think of that? For myself, I don't want to know. Just so long as it's happening." Without turning around, Emmanuel seems to guess that the pile of cookie boxes his younger son is stacking is about to fall. "Joseph, that's enough. Come and help me carry out the empty bottle returns." Over his shoulder he calls to Thomas, "You help the girl to what she wants."

As Thomas takes my money, I ask, "Where do you go to school?"

"Wayne State. I'm a sophomore in medical school and clerking at Receiving Hospital. I worked there this summer. Then, after another two years of medical school, I've got an internship and residency to get through. How about you?"

"I'm living with my father so I can go to art school."

"I'm sorry he's so sick. Advanced cirrhosis, he said." He gives me a hard look. "You knew what he has, didn't you? I hope I didn't speak out of turn."

"Actually I just found out." It's a relief to talk with someone about Dad, and Thomas seems really sympathetic. "It was kind of a shock," I admit. "I don't even really know what it means, and Dad won't say anything. I saw a letter that said he's stopped drinking though."

"For him, drinking would be fatal."

Fatal. That's such an ugly word. "What's going to happen to him?" Thomas looks away. I can tell he doesn't want to upset me. I say, "I'm the one who's going to take care of him, so I need to know." I *need* to know, but I don't want to know.

He sighs, but he tells me. "Unfortunately his liver is failing, Kate, and you can't get along without one. If he's stopped drinking, he could put in for a transplant."

"He already has, and he's been refused because of a heart problem." I told Thomas what the letter said.

"I'm afraid your dad will just get weaker then. You've probably noticed his yellow skin? That's jaundice. The main problem you have to look out for is fluid retention in his abdomen, which can be painful, and in his lungs, which can make it difficult to breathe." He sees how upset I'm getting and stops. "Sorry, I must sound like a textbook. I don't mean to overwhelm you. You were good to come to take care of him."

"I'll be at art school most of the time."

"Oh."

"What?"

"It's just that taking care of your dad might become a full-time job. But I'm sure you'll manage, and we'll be glad to help in any way we can. We like your dad."

Thomas expertly fits the chicken and the other groceries into a bag. He's probably had years of practice. He asks, "Do you know your way around Detroit?"

"Just how to get to school and back."

"Well, that's a start, at least. I'd like to be a help, but between school and the hospital and work here I don't have much time. Let me know, though, if you need help finding your way around, and I'll point you in the right direction."

"Thanks, I'll be fine."

He drops a chocolate bar into the bag. "We always give candy to the kids. It keeps them coming back."

As soon as I get home, I put the chicken in the oven with just a sprinkling of thyme and marjoram, a squirt or two of lemon, and a basting of butter. Mom's restaurant schedule means she's never home for meals, and when she is, she doesn't want to fool around with food. So she taught me how to cook at a young age, refusing to let me exist on pizza and SpaghettiOs. As I finish washing the lettuce for a salad, Dad wanders in and scrolls rapidly through his emails.

"You can answer these for me."

"How will I know what to say?"

"Just delete Julia's emails and tell all the art students wanting to know the secret of success to find their own way. You can inform any museums asking for loans of my paintings that currently all my work is at the Morgan Gallery in preparation for a show. Anything else, you can figure out yourself."

While the chicken bakes, I slog through the emails, including a lot of gushy ones, which require only a thanks, and one furious one accusing Dad of corrupting art. Finally there's a long email from Ian Morgan with questions about placement of paintings in the show, lighting, publicity, etc.

When I tell Dad, he says, "That can wait until next week."

"I can't do it next week. School starts. I'll be gone all day."

"School can wait. As long as you're down here, you may as well make yourself useful."

"I'm down here to go to art school."

"What makes you think you can paint?"

This is the chance I've been waiting for. I take the stairs two at a time, grab the small canvases I've brought with me, and do what I have longed to do ever since I walked into my father's house. I show him my work. These four small paintings are studies of the same maple tree at different seasons of the year. In the early spring the tree's buds are a purplish pink against a pale, late-afternoon lavender sky, the branches like interlocking arms. In summer the tree is crowded with leaves of a thick, rich green. In autumn the tree falls into a kaleidoscope of bits of color. The final painting is of a bare tree against white snow with two ominous-looking crows sitting in its branches. I painted it just after reading the lines in Shakespeare's sonnet, "boughs which shake against the cold, / Bare ruin'd choirs, where late the sweet birds sang." These paintings got me my scholarship, and I wait for Dad's approval, maybe even enthusiasm. I want him to say, "I'll take care of Morgan's email myself. School is more important."

Instead I get "Amateur work. Anyone with a decent

eye could do it. Are you telling me that *this* attempt at painting is more important than a major retrospective of my work?"

"I don't believe you!" I shout at him. I'm crushed, but I'm furious too. I fight back tears, refusing to give him the satisfaction of seeing me cry. I've been warned, haven't I? *Lethal selfishness* is what Mom always said he had.

Our silence screams at us all through dinner. We push our knives and forks around like weapons. There are no words of praise for the chicken or the salad made with my own special balsamic dressing. Dad eats almost nothing, in spite of the fact that it must be the first decent meal he's had since he left New York. When dinner is over, he disappears into his studio. I slam the dishes around in the sink. I have to get to art school, I tell myself. Just keep the goal in mind. Suck it up. I tell myself my father is just a selfish old man. He is wrong about my paintings. All he cares about is keeping me around to be his servant.

The next day I get out my map of the city and go online to find the schedules for the buses I'll need to take to school. Dad's car keys are on the kitchen counter, but I'm sure he won't let me use his car for something he doesn't want me to do, and I'm too proud to ask. I am a good driver, though. If you live in the country like I did, you drive a lot. Everything you need is a hundred miles away, over roads that stretch through miles of empty fields and woods. An old farmhouse or a sandy trail tells you where you are, not signposts and stoplights.

A friendly Detroit Department of Transportation website shows me routes, and I plot my course. One bus and a half dozen blocks of walking will do it.

I'm nervous about starting school. I look at my paintings again. After what Dad said about them, it's hard for me to get back my confidence. What if after all this I'm not an artist? I call Justin on my cell, needing to hear his voice. Before I left we talked about our future and decided we'd be best off as friends. Justin and I have a lot in common. We both know what we want to do with our lives, only I want to do it in Larch and Justin can't wait to leave Larch for some bigger city. We both believe we have a future, just not a future together.

"What's going on?"

Just the sound of his cheerful voice makes me feel better. "I'm afraid I've been kidding myself into thinking I'm an artist, and I'm not."

"What do you mean you're not an artist? Of course you are. You're going to be a star at that school. They certainly wouldn't have given you that scholarship if they didn't believe in you."

That's just what I need to hear. I chat with him about what his school is like and about his geeky roommate who is online all hours of the night playing chess with someone in Russia. When I hang up, things look better, and in a rush of energy I answer Dad's emails and turn the leftover chicken into potpies.

When I call him for supper, Dad snatches up his plate and takes it into the studio to eat and I'm left alone at the table. Fine with me. Evidently my cooking is going to be takeout.

After supper I walk up the street toward the store,

thinking maybe I'll see Thomas. But it's Sunday and the store is closed. I wander up and down the unfamiliar streets, looking in the lit windows of the houses, where families are sitting together talking or watching TV.

Later when I call Mom, I ask her about a serial we were watching.

"Doesn't he have a television?"

"No. Dad just paints. It doesn't matter—starting tomorrow I'll be busy with schoolwork."

"Kate, it's not too late to come home. You could take courses at the community college. They have a very good faculty."

"Mom, we've been over this. The time will go by fast."

"Fast for you. You'll be busy."

That hits me. Mom has never been the self-pitying kind. She must be really lonely. I want to tell her how much I miss her and how miserable I am, but I know that if I do, she'll make me come home. Tomorrow school starts and everything will be fine. "I love you," I tell Mom.

When she says good night, her voice shakes. Maybe I *should* go home. I don't know.

There's nothing left for me to do but get into bed. I don't hear Dad come upstairs. I decide he must be lost in his painting. I know the feeling. One idea after another grabs you and you can't bear to stop because you know the ideas might never come again. All the anger leaks out of me as I realize he's racing time.

In the morning I dress carefully for my first day at school, wondering what kids wear in the city, eventually pulling on my jeans and an old T-shirt. I'm there to learn to paint, not to make a fashion statement. I take a deep breath, suck in my stomach, zip my jeans, grab my backpack, and tiptoe down the stairway, anxious to get away before Dad is up. I feel like a captain deserting a ship. Don't I have a right to my own life? I promise myself I'll be especially nice to Dad in the afternoon when I get back.

As I leave, I lock the door behind me, shutting Dad and all the mean and selfish things he has said to me inside. I'm on my own. I'm not just my mom and dad's daughter. Today I'm whoever I decide I'm going to be. That's frightening. It's like when your canvas is empty and you know that your first line or your first splash of color will help set the course for what the painting will become. Today is the start of a new painting for me.

4

I had no idea the city could be so beautiful. In the creamy, golden light of the September morning all the grime of the city is swept clean. The old elm trees that yesterday looked diseased and faltering now appear brave and sturdy. Traffic that had been so overwhelming is cheerful and full of purpose. People know where they're going. On the bus everyone seems to welcome me, as if they have been waiting for me to join them. When I push through the doors of the school, I know I have my life back. I'm in exactly in the right place at exactly the right time. I want to grab hold of someone and say, *Isn't this great? Aren't you happy?* But I play it cool and just move along with the other kids, trying to look like it's nothing special. I'm relieved to see that almost everyone is wearing jeans. I think about how funny we'd look if God played a joke and suddenly made all the denim in the world disappear.

I have to ask where my first class is, and when I find the room, the students who are already there give me friendly, nervous smiles that say we're all in this together. English lit, the official start of my college career.

The professor says right away, "I know most of you resent having to sit through this class and would much rather be in a studio painting, but some of the best paintings have been done by artists inspired by great books or poems, just as some excellent books have been inspired by paintings. A single painting, Poussin's *A Dance to the Music of Time*, inspired Anthony Powell to write twelve terrific novels, hundreds of thousands of words." I try to look interested in this writer I've never heard of. The girl next to me rolls her eyes, and I grin.

Next up is art history class, where the professor is dressed in a long, flowing skirt that's been out of style since before I was born, but the skirt has patches of paint on it so I know she doesn't just talk about what she's teaching. Her voice is mesmerizing and intimate at the same time, as if she's talking just to me.

She shows us slides of still lifes with fruit and flowers and some paintings of landscapes by nineteenth-century American painters, each painting more lush and beautiful than the last. "All very pleasurable," she says, "but let's look at some work that shakes us up, that makes us turn away yet want to look at the same time. Let's talk about the beauty of ugliness."

A slide goes up of a couple sitting at a table looking starved and miserable. "Van Gogh," she says. "Notice how he's made use of the color blue to set the mood of the painting." Another slide. This one of a firing squad, officers aiming their guns at a row of prisoners. "Goya. You can see he spares us nothing. These are not easy artists." The next is a slide of a woman down on her knees scrubbing the floor of an empty office building, the darkness of the night leaking in through the windows. The woman's hair is hanging over her face, which has crumpled with fatigue and hopelessness. The painting is so depressing, I can hardly bear to look at it. A shiver goes through me. I know the artist.

"Dalton Quinn," the professor says. "He's a contemporary artist, still active but hasn't done much lately. Actually Quinn is rumored to be living right here in Detroit. Look at these paintings and see for yourselves how interesting ugliness can be if it's more than just ugliness, if the artist catches us up and makes us wonder about the people in his painting, makes us want to reach out to them."

My hand shoots up. "Why would an artist pick ugly things to paint when there's so much that's beautiful?" I want to know why my father's paintings are supposed to be great.

She looks surprised. "Are you saying there are no hungry people or countries where men are executed for their beliefs or women down on their knees scrubbing to earn a living?"

"No, but . . ." I was going to say, *I don't want to see them,* but that sounds stupid and selfish. "I just wondered . . ." I back off.

"You raise a good question. Remember there are many different ways of approaching truth." At the end of class the professor gives me an encouraging smile, as if to say there are no dumb questions.

At lunchtime I'm sitting alone in the cafeteria and I'm relieved when a girl from art history sits down next to me. I noticed her in my English class too. She's tall, nearly six feet, and thin, mostly legs. Her hair is trimmed close to her head, giving her an African queen profile. She's wearing an amazing outfit, a short black skirt and a long-sleeved purple silk blouse sewn with bright blue beads and cinched with a green belt. Her shoes have three-inch heels, as if to say, *You want tall. You've got it.*

She says, "I wanted to ask the same question you did. I'm glad you spoke up. Where're you from?"

"Northern Michigan," I say.

"So where are you living in Detroit?"

"I'm living in Hamtramck with my grandfather." The lie comes easily. I don't want questions about my dad. I don't want anyone finding out I'm Dalton Quinn's daughter.

"I'm from out of town too. Flint. Maybe we could get together and hang out. I don't know a soul here."

I hesitate, afraid to give her Dad's address. He'd be furious. He wouldn't want anyone in his house, certainly not an art student.

She notices the hesitation. "Your family doesn't want a big black girl hanging out in their neighborhood?"

"No, it's nothing like that. It's just that my grandfather is pretty sick. He's not up to having company."

"That's tough. I'm staying with my auntie, helping her with her sewing. She does alterations. She can stitch up anything. You should come over and see us. My auntie loves company. It gives her a chance to cook up a feast." She scrawls her address and her email and hands it to me, and I give her my cell number. "By the way, I'm Lila Brock."

"Kate Tapert."

"I'm not interested in being another van Gogh," Lila says. "I'm into fashion design. I'm going to get a job with *Vogue* and live in Paris and eventually I'll have my own atelier. Isn't that a gorgeous word?" She looks me over. "Kate, girl, you have got to break loose from the jeans and T-shirt mode. And what's with that braided leather belt? You've got a great body. Loosen up a little. And could you believe that professor with her hippie outfit? I'm going to wave a wand over her."

Lila and I sit next to each other in my afternoon life class, where you draw from models. "I told them I wanted to sketch people dressed, not naked," she says, "but they told me I have to understand how the body works, so I'll know how to hang clothes on it."

There's no model today. Instead we have a doctor from a nearby medical center with slides showing the body's insides, things like bones and muscles that you really don't want to think too much about. He tucks his glasses in his shirt pocket and sets up a real skeleton. We get a lecture on how Leonardo da Vinci spent hours on dissection before he began drawing the body. "You have to see what's underneath the flesh," the doctor says. "Actually, it would do you good to come over to the medical school and sit in on some dissection of cadavers. Thomas Eakins thought artists should observe surgeries and even perform dissections." He shows a slide of Eakins's famous painting *The Gross Clinic*, which depicts medical students watching the removal of a bone from a leg. Lila looks at me and pretends she's throwing up. Someone makes a joke about the name of the clinic. The professor hastily thanks the doctor, cutting off the chatter, and promises us he'll have a model the next day. "A live one." He winks.

At supper that night I can't keep still, I'm so excited about my first day. I tell Dad, "I've never been around kids my own age who actually care about art, who want to live and breathe it. We're all there for the same purpose, and who knows, maybe one of us will go on to be famous. And I met this great girl who's so funny and friendly. She wants to be a dress designer. A doctor came and showed us a real skeleton. All the professors were great, and one of them showed us a painting of yours! It was the one of the scrubwoman. I didn't say anything about you being my dad, because I know you don't want publicity. She talked about how it has the beauty of ugliness."

Dad puts down his spoonful of chili. "You're paying money to have someone tell you what my painting means when I'm right here?"

I quibble. "I'm not paying money. I'm on a scholarship. Anyhow, aren't you interested in what people think of your painting?"

"The last thing an artist should be thinking about is what someone thinks of his painting. You're like a kindergartner coming home with stories about playing ring-around-the-rosy, Kate. I don't want to hear another word about your school." He pushes his half-full bowl of chili away as if it has been poisoned and gets up from the table. Before he heads into his studio, he says, "I'm going to ask Morgan for another advance on my work. It can pay for a dorm room for you at your precious school. That will solve both of our problems."

I'm stunned. For a minute I consider taking the money and getting out. All these years Dad hasn't given me a cent, and I'm certainly due a little help from him. I'd have a place to live with the other kids, and he'd have this place to himself. But I'd lose my chance to get to know my father, even if knowing him is all misery and punishment. And if he gets sicker, who will take care of him?

After supper I call Justin and tell him what's happened. "Sure," he says. "Take the money and run. You don't owe him anything."

"But he's not well. He might need me."

"You shouldn't let that interfere with your dreams. I thought you wanted to be an artist."

"I want to be a human being too."

"Look, I've got a lot of homework for tomorrow.

I'm really sorry you've got this creep for a father, but it seems to me you're getting all tangled up in his problems. You've got to keep your eye on your goal."

"You're probably right," I tell him.

By the time I dial Mom, I've all but decided to live in a dorm. But how will I explain that to her? What will she say when I tell her I'm accepting money from Dad? I hope she'll just be glad that I won't be under the same roof with him anymore.

Mom doesn't answer. Then I remember it's Monday night, her bridge night. I think about what it's like when it's her turn to have her friends at our trailer, the four women crowded around our little table, laughing and gossiping, talking about where the sales are and what their kids are doing, drinking cups of coffee and eating the double chocolate brownies Mom always makes.

The thought of the brownies makes me hungry. When I wander downstairs to get some peanut butter and crackers, I hear Dad talking to Morgan. He's saying that he'll be sending a couple of paintings soon and is asking for the money. I hear his angry voice: "What do you mean I've had my last advance? I'll be sending the paintings any day now." There are more angry words, but I don't stay to listen.

I forget about the dorm.

5

Every day at school is amazing. Not just classes. Yesterday a local rock group came to play in the cafeteria during lunch, and we were beating time with our silverware and dancing around. Today there was a Ping-Pong competition and a free yoga class. Lila showed me the fitness room, and we worked out on the bikes, her long legs going a mile a minute.

The weather has been warm, and between classes or at lunchtime we all hang out in the courtyard like living statues scattered among the famous sculptures. Everyone talks with everyone else because we're all interested in the same thing—creative ideas to put down on paper or turn into clay or glass or paintings or even automobiles. There's a student from Japan who told me he has this idea for a car that will work on the rubber-band principle. He tried to explain it and totally lost me, but then I got him talking about the island in Japan where he came from. It's mostly sea and mountains, and I could tell he was a little lonesome for it, like I'm lonesome for up north.

One afternoon Lila dragged me over to a guy who was wearing an amazing T-shirt. She practically attacked him. "I'm going to pull that shirt right off your beautiful body and steal it if you don't tell me where you got it."

"Made it."

"You didn't!"

"I did. I dyed it and then I buried it and then I ran my car over it."

"It's too cool." Lila got right in his face. "I've got a proposition. I'm going to have a little atelier of my own soon, nothing fancy, but I could sell as many of those shirts as you can run over."

"Deal."

It was like that all the time. New ideas floating around everywhere, even in the computer room where I checked Dad's emails for him. Sitting right next to me one afternoon was a girl with the most incredible designs popping up on her screen. I just sat there looking, excited to see what was coming next. "You can do that on a computer?" I asked.

"Sure. Like this." She started to explain, but it was over my head. Still, kids were happy to let you in on their secrets because they knew someone else would let them in. I loved that.

There is so much to discover. There are the kilns, the big ovens that bake the clay pots, and a room with furnaces where you can twist molten glass into any shape you want. All the classrooms have huge windows, so the city is as much inside the school as out. You never forget your connection with it for a minute. I think we all know Detroit is in trouble: empty houses and stores, jobs lost . . . but we're the new wave. We're going to make it better. We're going to put Detroit back on the map.

Yesterday it was still warm and almost like summer, but this morning there was a cold rain that told me September is nearly over. I can't believe how fast the month has gone. After class I know I should hurry home and see how Dad is. I also know Dad will have his usual sarcastic remark about my wasting my time at school, and I'm not quite ready for that today. Instead I stop at an art-supply store and pick up some boards to gesso. What you do is sort of whitewash the boards to make a background for the paint. I linger over the rows of paint tubes; they're as beautiful to me as a Dior dress would be to Lila, and practically as expensive. I buy a tube of Naples yellow and one of medium magenta. I have ideas just thinking of the colors, and I'm eager to get started with the painting. On the bus on the way home I go over everything that happened in school that day, not wanting to let it go. Since I have school, I know I can put up with Dad and his demands.

When I get home, I find the house empty. In a way I'm relieved, even glad. I'll have the peace and quiet I need to get my boards prepared for painting. But a whisper in the back of my head repeats, *Something's wrong.* Dad is weak, and walking is hard for him, and the car is in the driveway. So where is he? Dad is more of a distraction when he's gone than when he's here. I put down my backpack and head out, wandering up and down the nearby streets. I even check the convenience store, but Emmanuel says he hasn't seen Dad in days and gives me a critical look that says, *How can you not know where your father is? What kind of daughter are you?*

Finally I head back home, and I'm opening the jar of gesso when the phone rings. "Is this Kate Quinn, Mr. Quinn's daughter?" Kate Quinn. No one has called me that in years. My first impulse is to say no. "Hello," the voice says. "Are you there?"

"This is Kate Quinn," I say. I have a feeling these are the most dangerous words I have ever uttered.

"This is the emergency room at Detroit Receiving Hospital. Don't be alarmed. Your father is fine. He just had a little trouble breathing. Luckily he had his cell with him and called 911. We didn't want to send him home until we knew someone would be there." The voice develops a scolding tone. "In his condition he needs someone to keep an eye on him. Do you want to pick him up, or should we send him home in an ambulance?"

"I'll be right there," I say.

The car keys are still on the kitchen counter. My hands are shaking so much, I have trouble digging out my map of Detroit. I find the little red crosses on the map that show where the hospitals are. Receiving isn't far. I'm furious with myself and with Dad all at the same time. Knowing how sick he is, I should have checked on him before I left for school today. But wasn't he alone before I arrived? Why couldn't he just let me get on with my life? Was he doing this to punish me for going off to school?

I leave the car in the emergency parking lot and

rush into the hospital. All the chairs in the emergency room are filled, and a few people who look like they should be sitting are leaning against the wall. I have never been in a hospital. Everything is strange: the smell, the doctors in white coats with stethoscopes hanging around their necks like some sort of weird necklaces, the moan coming from behind a curtain strung across a cubicle. I'm told someone will see me shortly. Minutes later Thomas appears. At first I don't recognize him in his white jacket. "You're in uniform," I say to cover my nervousness.

"It's to keep the patients from learning we're just students. I'm sorry about your dad. When I saw his name, I had a talk with the doctor who examined him. He was having trouble breathing and they removed fluid from his lungs; that's all part of his illness. He'll be fine now, at least for a while, but it may happen again. He needs to tell you when he's beginning to have trouble so it doesn't become an emergency." Thomas gives me a professional look. "You all right?"

"I'm fine. I know you told me that could be a

problem, but I didn't think it would happen so soon."

"I'm afraid the cirrhosis is pretty far along, and I noticed a little disorientation when I talked with him." He sees my questioning look. "If you're going to be at school, you should think about getting someone in to be with him while you're away, and I'll put in a request for a visiting nurse to stop by once a week to see how he's getting along." He puts an arm around my shoulders and gives a reassuring squeeze. I lean into him and grit my teeth to keep from crying. Why does someone being nice to you make you want to cry?

Thomas heads down a hall and is back a minute later with Dad, who is struggling to get out of his wheelchair. "Sorry, Mr. Quinn," Thomas says in a firm voice, "I have orders to deliver you to your car in the chair. It's hospital routine." He tries to make a joke. "I don't want you suing me or anything."

Dad glares at me. "Don't just stand there—get the car."

When I drive up, Thomas helps Dad into the front seat next to me.

"Let's go," Dad orders.

I pull away while Thomas stands there watching us.

When we arrive home and I've settled Dad in, I say, "I think we should get a nurse's aide to stay with you during the day. I'll be here weekends and evenings."

"A babysitter? Over my dead body. I thought that's what you were here for."

"I'm here to go to school. Remember?"

He cuts me off. "I can't afford help. Morgan isn't going to give me another cent until I finish my paintings and ship them off."

"How can you not have any money? You're famous."

"I *was* famous. I created myself and then I destroyed myself. I promised work for a show, or a painting for a museum, but then I didn't deliver. Killed my reputation. Booze, women, traveling, that's all I cared about. I thought I had all the time in the world. Now I only have one chance left.

"When the doctors gave me my diagnosis, I stopped drinking, did two paintings, and showed them to Morgan. I promised enough new things for a show and he agreed. I rented this house a year ago, and it's a race—my liver against enough work to get my reputation back. You've got the rest of your life, Kate. I've got months."

As if to prove his point, Dad refuses to lie down and goes into his studio instead, slamming the door behind him.

I go to my room and try to figure out what to do. I don't want to give up school to take care of Dad. I don't think I can do it. Maybe I should leave. I could go back home and get a job, save my money, and come back to school in a year or two when I have enough money for a dorm room.

Then that whisper in the back of my head starts up again. Who is it that sics that little voice on you that insists you do the opposite of what you want? The one that makes you miserable until you do it? *He's your father,* the voice says. *He's an old man and he's dying. Just take care of him.* My father has led this perfectly disgusting life, and the little voice is going to make *me* be the one to pay for it. I guess I have to remember that part of my coming down was to get to know this man, for better or worse. Just because it was harder than I ever thought it would be doesn't mean I should give up. Especially when he needs me.

I stick my backpack and books in the empty space where the dresser drawer is missing. I cry, wallowing in my disappointment, taking a bath in a big tub of warmed-up frustration. *All right,* I tell the voice, *I'll quit school. For now.* But I promise myself it won't be forever. At least I'll be near school. Lila will tell me what's going on, and the Art Institute is nearby. I'll take care of Dad, but I won't stop painting. I'll find a place where I can work. Dad can't begrudge me that, because if I'm not painting, I'm not alive. He'll understand that.

There's a third bedroom at the back of the house. It's filled with a jumble of boxes that evidently Dad never got around to unpacking. There are no curtains on the windows, and the last of the afternoon sun is leaking into the room. I tackle the boxes and clear some space. Just accomplishing that much makes me feel better, as if the boxes were problems that I've now stacked out of the way. While Dad is working, I'll be upstairs painting, forgetting that I'm marooned in the middle of a strange city with someone who can barely stand me and who I dislike more every minute.

After dinner I write a letter to the school explaining that family circumstances prevent me from continuing the semester. I thank them for the scholarship, tell them I'm sure it will benefit another student, and apologize for any trouble I have caused them. I say I hope they will allow me to return to school sometime in the future. I remember all the soppy romance novels I've read where tears drop on a letter the heroine is writing, and find out it happens in real life too. Before I can change my mind, I hurry out to mail the letter. In one big bite the mailbox swallows up the envelope and all my dreams.

6

The next morning I picture my art school classmates heading to their first class. In the life class they'll have a new live model to sketch. In our lit class they'll be reading Shakespeare's *Hamlet*. We were not only supposed to read the play but apply some aspect of our art to it. Lila was doing costumes. I was sketching out the sets—all those gloomy castle scenes with black skeletonlike trees disappearing in the fog. There was going to be a band playing after school, and I had a sort of date to see them with Nick, who does amazing sculptures from junk he picks up on the streets or finds in trash barrels. But I won't be there. I'll be right here taking care of Dad.

I can hear Mom whispering in my ear, *I told you it was all about him*. I almost bolt out the door, but I don't.

Dad comes down for breakfast and looks around, as if he isn't sure where he is or who I am. I remember what Thomas said about Dad being disoriented. He holds his toast in one hand and his knife in the other like he has no idea what to do with either of them. I begin to feel confused myself. Where is this going? I hand him the butter, and after a minute he seems fine, finishing breakfast and taking his coffee into the studio with him. There is no word about my not returning to school, no thanks, and no apology. He just accepts the fact that he comes first. That's the way it is in his world and I'd better get used to it.

I hurry through the dishes, swishing them in the hot, soapy water, rinsing them and leaving them in the rack to dry. When I open the back door to take out the trash, the gray-and-white feral cat I've seen prowling around the neighborhood runs off. It doesn't have a home, but I don't feel sorry for it because the cat can do just as it likes. A waft of fresh air makes me want to go for a long walk, all the way to northern Michigan. Instead I head for my own little studio to get to work. Driving home from the hospital the day before, I began thinking about the challenge of painting trees in the darkness, and I'm anxious to solve the problem.

As I pass Dad's studio, I hear something that sounds like crying. Every sensible impulse tells me to just hurry up the stairs, but my feet are stuck. The next thing I know, I'm knocking on the studio door. No response. Is he okay? What if Dad's too sick to come to the door? When I look in, I find him crumpled in a chair, his shoulders shaking. I have never seen a man cry. Men are supposed to handle everything. That's what they're there for. I put a hand on his shoulder.

He shakes it off. "Just leave me alone." He blows his nose with incredible force. "You can call Morgan and tell him the show is off."

"What do you mean?" I look around the studio.

There are a half dozen canvases stacked against the walls. Several obviously need work. One stands on an easel. I try to think of something encouraging. "You said you've already sent some work to the gallery, and when you finish these, you'll have more than enough work for a show."

I go from painting to painting, telling Dad how great each one is. And they are. It's true there's a lot of ugliness, but they're strong and shout for your attention.

As I explain his own work to him, Dad stares at me as if I'm translating a foreign language. He grunts. "You don't know what you're talking about. Make me some more coffee. I suppose you can manage that?"

I go out to the kitchen to make him coffee, and when I get back he's working. I think about going upstairs to my own work, but I've lost the urgency. I've given Dad my enthusiasm and now I don't have any left. Shouldn't it be the other way around? Shouldn't the father be the one in charge? Shouldn't he be the one to encourage me? But I know this isn't going to change. It'll be a race for Dad to finish his work while he's still able to paint, and I'll have to be cheerleader as well as housekeeper and nurse.

In the late afternoon the doorbell rings. A large woman stands there, solid as stone. With her dark suit and black bag she looks forbidding, but I notice she is wearing fanciful earrings that are a dangle of little hearts. She asks, "Is this Dalton Quinn's house? I'm Erlita Parker, the visiting nurse."

"I'm Mr. Quinn's daughter, Kate. Come on in. Let me talk with my dad."

I go into Dad's studio. He gives me a furious look. "What do you want?"

"The visiting nurse is here."

"Get rid of her."

"I'm afraid he won't see you," I tell Erlita.

"Honey, you looked wiped out. Better let me in to see for myself."

"Is she gone?" Dad shouts.

Erlita motions in the direction of the studio. "He's in there?"

I nod.

"Sounds cranky." She walks past me and into the studio.

Dad stares at Erlita. "Who are you and what the devil do you think you're doing here?" He turns to me. "I told you to get that woman out of here."

Erlita introduces herself.

"The last thing I need is some officious nurse telling me what to do. I didn't ask for you and I don't want you."

Erlita looks around. "My, you must be an artist. Why don't you paint something pretty? I wouldn't have one of those on my walls."

Dad goes through a string of curses, some of which are new to me, but Erlita stands her ground. She says, "Those bad words are like vipers issuing out of your mouth. Don't you know what the Bible has to say about such language? And in front of your girl. You ought to be ashamed. Now I'm here to check your lungs and that's what I'm going to do. I guess you want to get back to your painting, but unless you let me do my job, you aren't going to have many painting days left, and if I were you, with a mouth like that, I wouldn't be too anxious to meet my maker."

Dad spits out, "If you think you're getting any money from me, I can tell you that even if I had it, I wouldn't pay you a cent. So you can just clear out."

"That's not a problem. The hospital made arrangements for these visits. Believe me, they don't want to see you back there anytime soon. Now if you'll just be quiet." Erlita gets out a blood-pressure cuff and a stethoscope. I hold my breath.

Erlita looks over at me. "Honey, why don't you get me a nice cold glass of water? I've been running all morning."

I return to find Dad is lying down. When she's finished, I accompany Erlita to the door. "How did you get him to agree to the examination?"

"I treated him just like I do my five-year-old—let him get it all out of his system and then close in for the kill. What you've got to realize is that your dad is scared. He knows he doesn't have a lot of time left. Now what about you? You making some time for yourself, honey?"

She puts her arm around me and that's too much. It's like my mom being there, and I haven't realized how much I miss Mom and how much I need her. I lose it, and the next thing I know, I'm crying into Erlita's shoulder and she's patting me on the back.

"Anytime you want to slip out, he'll be fine for a couple of hours on his own. I'll tell you what I'll do," she says. "We don't live too far from here. I'll send my little girl by to give you a night off. You don't have to pay her a cent. She belongs to our church's Good Deed Girls, and she needs the credit. Her name is Ruth after the lady in the Bible. She's a little thing, not big like me, but I taught her not to be afraid of anything and she isn't. I'll be back at the end of the week, and you can call me anytime." She thrusts a card with her phone number in my hand and she's gone.

I hurry up to my studio, clutching Erlita's card. An hour ago I had never heard of her. Now she's the most important person in my life. All it took was a few words. Dad will hang on to me and I'll hang on to Erlita and maybe neither of us will drown.

★ ★ ★

When I'm painting, there's no time or place. It's nearly suppertime, and except for a quick lunch I've been at it all day. When my cell rings, it pulls me out of a trance and for a minute I don't know where I am. It's Mom. "So are you all right?" she asks.

"Yes," I say. And I am. I always am when I'm painting. Wonderful as it is to hear Mom's voice, I'm almost sorry to have to put down my brush. A quick and awful thought shoots through my head. Maybe I'm more like my dad than I want to be: painting before people.

"How's school?" Mom asks.

I think fast. If I tell Mom the truth, she'll have a fit. She'll say Dad ruined her life and now he's ruining mine and I have to come home right away. She won't really care what happens to Dad, only to me.

"The school is great," I say. Not a complete lie.

"And what about him?"

"He's fine," I say.

I tell her about Lila, and she says it's nice I have a

friend. She tells me there's a big scandal at the resort where she works in the restaurant. The restaurant manager ran off with the owner's wife. Except that turns out to be good news, because they gave Mom the manager's job. "Only temporary," she says, but I hear hope and pride in her voice.

She wants to know if I have the right clothes and if the neighborhood is safe and if I'm getting enough sleep.

"Love you," she says.

"Love you," I answer. We sign off. I don't like lying to Mom, but I can't desert Dad. Things are getting so complicated. I wish I had someone to talk it all over with. I think about Thomas and wonder when I'll see him again.

I heat up soup and make Dad sandwiches with leftover chicken, cutting off the crusts like you're supposed to do for invalids. I slice the sandwiches into small triangles so they look appetizing and take them into the studio, because he won't come out. He barely notices me, waving the plate away. I leave it on a table and back away like I'm trying to entice a wild animal. I pause for a minute to look at what Dad's working on. It's a man and a woman standing in a darkened room. They're facing away from each other, the man looking out one window, the woman out the other. They are together in separate worlds. It's night in the painting, and from the windows you see trees, their leafy crowns huddled together as if they need to be protected from the darkness around them. I say this to Dad.

He turns away from the canvas and looks at me like he's seeing me for the first time. "Protected from the darkness. That's rather good. Actually it's how you see trees at night, as masses because you can't see the daylight coming through the interstices."

"Interstices?"

"The spaces between something, like the spaces between the branches. At night there are no visible spaces."

How to paint trees at night is the very problem I've been thinking about. I realize my painting and Dad's have come together, and it gives me a little shiver of pleasure. I'd like to tell him, but he grabs a triangle of chicken sandwich and turns back to his painting. I'm dismissed, but I don't care. We have just had our first intelligent conversation. And it was about painting. I go upstairs and look at my night trees again. I pick up my brush.

At midnight I'm awakened by a call from Justin. He's been up late studying for a test. He tells me he's in an advanced math class and has met two students there who have an old hunting cabin outside of town in the woods. He's up there for the weekend. Porcupines gnaw on their cabin, deer graze on nearby fields, and yesterday they saw an eagle. On quiet nights they can hear the foghorn warning ships on Lake Superior. It's like Justin and I are living in different countries. After I hang up, I decide I'll get some cat food for the feral cat. I need something wild near me.

7

*T*wo weeks go by before I feel it's safe to leave Dad for a couple of hours. It's been like house arrest. I wish I could walk out the door into my beloved woods instead of into the city, but truthfully any change of scenery is welcome at this point. Stepping outside, I see the cat has rejected the food I set out. Why would it want to belong to someone when it can go its own way? I don't blame it. In the mild October afternoon I wander in the direction of the convenience store. In front of the store I spot Thomas getting out of a car.

"How's your dad?"

I give him all the news and tell him about Erlita.

"So what are you doing?"

"I'm out for a walk. Erlita says it's all right to leave Dad for a couple of hours. I'm hungry for a little country, but I guess I'll never find it here."

"My head's full of comparative anatomy and I could use a breather myself. Hop in—I'll show you countryside."

He opens the car door, shoving aside a bird's nest of books, newspapers, and empty coffee cups. The car coughs and hesitates and then does what it's told. As we drive away, I see Emmanuel peering out the store window. And he's frowning.

"Your dad doesn't look too pleased. Were you supposed to be doing something?"

"No. Nothing to worry about."

"Maybe he doesn't approve of me."

"He likes you . . . but he doesn't like the combination of you and me. He thinks that I should be studying and that you're not one of us."

"Us?"

"Chaldean."

"Isn't that a narrow point of view?"

"Not if you know my dad's history. Dad came here from Iraq in the sixties, when he was just a boy, after Saddam killed his dad and his uncle. He's never really recovered from that. He and his mother and grandparents were brought over by some relatives, but we still have family who left Iraq and are living in Lebanon and who desperately want to come here. It's my duty to be successful and to make some money so we can help them like someone helped us. There's no place in that plan for me to get diverted by girls who aren't Chaldean."

"But if your family has been here since the sixties . . ."

"Oh, we're integrated, we're part of the city's multicultural mix and all that, but Dad has a lot of respect for the old traditions. He doesn't want us to lose our identity. Anyhow, he's got nothing to worry about, since the last thing I'm interested in is getting involved with someone."

So I'm warned. "Don't you resent having to do what your family wants?"

"Nah. I'm happy studying medicine. The rest of the stuff I try not to think about."

"At least you get to go to school." My voice catches in my throat. I can't help it.

Thomas puts his hand on my shoulder and pats me like you would a kid. "Kate, I really admire what you're doing. If it's any comfort, your father doesn't have long."

Strangely that's no comfort at all, and I have to grit my teeth and hold my breath to keep from breaking out in sobs. I blink and concentrate on the view out the car window. I don't think this is what Thomas meant, but I'm beginning to see countryside sneaking into the city. There are empty lots where houses have been torn down, and Queen Anne's lace, knapweed, wild asters, and goldenrod are blooming in the lots. The country is taking over the city.

When I ask about the empty lots, Thomas says, "Urban prairie. Houses were abandoned and then used as drug houses. Eventually they burned down or were torn down by the city as a nuisance."

A few miles away is a large medical complex. Thomas shows me the medical school, and I'm happy that he wants to share his world. Then we head east and cross a bridge over the Detroit River. BELLE ISLE, the sign says. Beautiful Island. The island, a couple of miles long, is a kind of wilderness inhabited mainly by Canada geese with their long black necks and white chin straps. Flocks and flocks of them are on the grass and swimming in the river and in the canals that wind through the island. Some of them might be the same geese that fly over our trailer up north and nest in a nearby lake. I envy them their freedom to go where they want to.

"Belle Isle is crowded with people in the summertime," Thomas says. "On hot nights families come here and camp out to get a little cool air from the river." From the island you can see an impressive outline of Detroit's downtown, the tall buildings resting against blue sky. In the distance is the bridge from Detroit to Windsor in Canada. In minutes you can be in another country, and I wonder how that would feel.

On this October afternoon we seem to be alone on the island. It's a ghost park. Scattered through the woods are the black skeletons of dead trees. Along the canals the tangled boughs of ancient willows blow in the breeze. There are empty picnic tables and a deserted playground, the orphaned swings moving in the wind. I resolve to come back here and do some sketches for a painting.

"This is where I do my thinking," Thomas says.

"What do you think about?"

He's quiet and I'm afraid I'm being nosy, but after a minute he takes a long breath like he's getting ready to plunge into the deep end of a pool. "My father wants me to marry a girl who recently came over from Lebanon. She got in with a student visa. She's a trained scientist and is doing graduate work. If I marry her, she'll be a U.S. citizen. That will help her to bring over her brothers and sisters. Like our family, they're refugees from Iraq and living in Lebanon. Mary's a very nice girl, and Dad's not pushing it, but I can feel the pressure."

"It sounds like we're both getting pressured to do the right thing, even when we don't want to."

"It's different for you. Your life will only be on hold for a short time with your father. If I get married, that's a lifetime."

We circle the island and then turn toward home. I'm thinking of what's ahead for Dad, and I say, "Doctors must have to get used to the idea of a patient's death. How do you do it?"

"It's not easy. The longer you've treated a patient and the better you know the patient, the harder it is. And sometimes it doesn't take that long to form a bond; a patient will just grab you. When I was on duty in the oncology clinic I had a boy with a brain tumor and very little chance of making it. He was the same age as my brother. He was a baseball freak and we'd talk about the Tigers every day and argue about the batting lineup. If I had some extra time, I'd watch the game with him on the TV he had in his room, and I bought him a Tigers cap to wear over his bandages. I haven't been able to watch a game since he died.

"I'm not going to tell you it will be easy with your dad, Kate. The longer you stay here, the more you do for him, the more you'll be invested in keeping him with you. So you're taking a chance. You're making it hard on yourself."

"Are you saying I should go home?"

"That's up to you. I'm just trying to prepare you."

I still think there must be some way of protecting myself. Some way to make this easier. I resolve to be impersonal, like a nurse taking care of a patient. Make it a job. Keep my distance. I'll keep reminding myself that for years Dad had nothing to do with me. There's no reason why I should lose sleep over him. But I don't know. Somehow I don't think that's going to work.

Thomas drops me off in front of Dad's house, and I thank him for the great afternoon. I've told him about Ruth and the Good Deed Girls, so before he drives away, he leans out of the car and says, "Get your Good Deed Girl to stay Saturday night and I'll show you my favorite part of the city."

"That would be great," I say, and begin making

plans for my first Detroit date.

Back inside I check to see if Dad is working, and he is. He hasn't even missed me. That's fine. We'll be like those planets in their own orbits. I go into the kitchen and spend an hour laboring over my special minestrone, made with lots of veggies. That will be nourishing for Dad. When I'm finished I make custard, even more nourishing. If I keep him alive, I won't have to worry about death.

8

*D*ad doesn't get up today. When I take him breakfast, he waves it away, keeping only the coffee. I notice that his skin, and even the whites of his eyes, is tinted pale yellow like a late-afternoon sun. Cadmium yellow light hue to cadmium yellow medium. "How do you feel?" I ask, and he responds by ordering me out of the room.

I call Erlita's cell. "That's just part of the illness, honey. You got to expect ups and downs. He short of breath?"

I think of how he shouted at me. "No," I say.

"That's good. I'll be by tomorrow."

I want to get out my paints, but somehow Dad's not painting makes it impossible for me to work as well. It's like we're tied together. I don't want that. I get busy with Dad's emails. I compose an encouraging reply to Ian Morgan's one-word query, "When?" by telling him Dad's making great progress, but he wants everything to be perfect. Immediately Morgan shoots back an answer as if he had been sitting at his computer waiting for my response. Maybe he has. "I'm not interested in perfection," he sends. "I'm interested in the art of the possible."

I check the back porch. The cat food is gone this morning, and I see tufts of cat hair caught on the mat outside the door. I don't know why I'm so pleased.

Dad's back in his studio. He hasn't bothered to shave and he's barefoot. I tell him what Morgan said. "Can't we just send a couple of pictures to keep him satisfied?" I ask.

"They're not ready."

I know he'll be furious with me, but I home in on

two paintings that look finished. "Why couldn't you send these?"

"If you think you can tell me when I'm finished with a painting, you can go back to your wilderness." But I see he's considering what I've said. He goes up to his room and comes back with a fleece jacket.

Dad says, "If you're so anxious to send these off, you can give me a hand." I take one painting and he takes the other himself, shuffling ahead of me to the garage, where he's set up a kind of carpentry shop.

"When you start out," Dad says, "you'd better be able to knock your own frames together and know how to ship your pictures. There won't be any money to have someone do it for you."

I'm amazed he's talking with me as if I'm really going to be an artist one day and need to know these things. Is he actually taking me seriously?

We wrap the two paintings carefully and crate them. I hand and hold. He pounds and saws. He likes what he's doing, and I remember he started out as a carpenter during his early years in construction. What would have happened if he'd kept on with that instead of becoming an artist? Would building a house give him the same satisfaction as completing a painting? Just before he pounds in the final nail, he has a change of heart. "Maybe I should take the one of the parking lot back to the studio. I'm not sure." I want to stop him, but what if he's right and I'm wrong? He reaches for a crowbar to pry open the crate, but he's exhausted and can't find the strength to pick it up. "Running on empty," he says. "Send them off." He disappears into the house.

After they're labeled, I call for a pickup and email Ian Morgan: "Two paintings on their way, and they're fabulous."

The answer comes back. "'Fabulous'? We're not talking about a new pair of shoes. Excellent or well-done, perhaps. Surely your father's work deserves a more exact description."

I send off: "Alarming, terrifying, the world we refuse to see."

Back comes: "No need to overdo."

I check on Dad. He's sound asleep. When I bring his supper up to him, I have a hard time waking him. Then he grumbles about everything. He says, "I'm not hungry. Take the food away. It's too hot in here. Open a window. Stop hovering."

I bite my tongue and get out of there. He's asleep again before I close the door.

In the morning when I look in on him, I freeze. There's blood all over his pillow. "Just a nosebleed," he says, and tells me to get out. Maybe I should call Thomas and cancel Saturday night, but I don't want to stop having something to look forward to.

When Erlita comes, Dad's had two cups of coffee and some toast. He's hard at work in the studio. After checking on him, she finds me in the kitchen and answers my questions. "Nosebleeds aren't unusual with this, and neither is sleepiness. A little more jaundice, but that's to be expected. Now, I haven't forgotten you. My girl is all set to come and sit with your daddy. When do you want her?"

I hold my breath. "Could she come Saturday night?"

"You've got it. And don't you worry. That little girl can handle anything that comes her way. I taught her well. I don't want her out late, though. We go to early service Sunday."

I paw through my clothes. Pathetic. We never dress up at home. A night out might mean a blouse with your jeans instead of a T-shirt, but that's it. I scoop up the possibilities and head for Lila's.

Lila lives in the back of a storefront that has an ALTERATIONS sign hanging in the window. The sign is carefully lettered and decorated with flowers and birds. Lila must have done it. Inside there are racks of clothes her aunt, Ernestine, is working on. The clothes on one rack look sad and hopeful at the same time, as if they're waiting for Lila's aunt to perform a miracle. On the second rack the clothes appear happier, with shorter hems and the wrinkles ironed out. Aunt Ernestine greets me like a long-lost daughter and brings Lila and me cookies and milk. She's wearing a pincushion tied to her arm and a tape measure around her neck. After she leaves us, I can hear the hum of her serger.

"You've got yourself a date? And you're wearing that?" Lila shakes her head. "What else you got?" She snatches a denim skirt from the pitiful collection I've brought. "Let's see." Lila empties out a drawer and retrieves a spool of lace, which she pins along the hem so it looks like there's a petticoat underneath the skirt. She takes a T-shirt and cuts a scoop neck, then gathers the waist. More lace. While Auntie is stitching it all up, Lila borrows her scissors and goes for my hair. I scream and run, but she chases me around the room. "You've got great hair, but no one can tell if you just pull it back and tie it up like it's been kidnapped."

I sigh and close my eyes.

"What's going on at school?" I want to know and I don't want to know.

"Halloween's next week, so we had a pumpkin-carving contest. You wouldn't believe how much work everyone put into them. So creative. So much fun.

There were prizes, and then we took them to a children's shelter." She sees the look of longing on my face. "You start thinking up a good idea for next year, girl. I just know your grandfather's going to get better."

My hair falls softly around my face, and when I try on the skirt and blouse, I feel transformed. Lila wants to lend me a pair of her four-inch heels, but when I put them on, I wobble and nearly fall over. I promise not to wear my flip-flops though. "And get some polish on those naked toes," Lila orders. "They're embarrassing."

I hug her and then Aunt Ernestine. I promise to call Lila and let her know how the date goes. I tell them that in exchange for all they've done for me, I'll bring them a painting.

That Saturday night when I open the front door, there is this tiny, incredibly neat girl, a kind of miniature that you'd keep on a shelf or dangling from a bracelet. She has on a white blouse, with tiny ruffled cuffs around tiny wrists, and a pleated skirt, each pleat perfectly creased. This is never going to work. Dad will brush her away like a bit of fluff. Disappointed, I try to think of polite words to send her on her way, but she walks right up to me, her little shoes tap-tapping, her hand outstretched. I'm actually afraid to close my hand over hers; I might crush it. But her grasp is strong.

"I want you to know," she says, "how much I appreciate that I can help you out. Momma told me your daddy is a famous artist." She thrusts a notebook at me. "Could you please sign me in? I've got to keep track of my hours. And don't worry, Momma gave me all the phone numbers in case of an emergency."

"I'm afraid this isn't going to work out, Ruth," I say. "My father is a handful, more than you'll be able to manage."

As if to prove my point, Dad flings open the studio door. "I told you I won't . . ." His mouth snaps shut. Gently he pushes Ruth into his studio and arranges her on a chair. "Sit right there and don't move."

"Yes, sir." She seems perfectly content to follow his odd orders.

He gives me a quick glance. "Get out," he says. "We don't need you."

Should I leave Ruth with my dad, the artist who turns everything ugly? Ruth is giving Dad a beatific smile. I think she figures she'll get extra points for this.

Before I can debate further, Thomas is at the door. There's a startled look on his face; then he smiles and says, "What happened to the other Kate?"

I realize he hasn't seen me in anything but an old T-shirt and jeans with my hair pulled back. "It's just me," I assure him, and wriggle my painted toes in the sandals I found at a secondhand store.

I squeeze into his ancient car, which is shuddering and panting like an old dog. Now that we're no longer just a couple of people who ran into each other, both of us are embarrassed and too quiet and then too talkative. We head downtown and park in a lot that borders the river. There are hundreds of people strolling up and down a walk that runs along the river's edge. There are a lot of kids and toddlers in strollers.

A Mexican band is playing salsa. Thomas buys us hot dogs and we sit on a bench and eat them while watching the small boats on the river. The people on the boats wave like mad to the people on shore, and we all wave back. Tonight we are all friends.

When you like someone, you want to bring them into your life, to hurry and tell them all about yourself and find out everything about them. Thomas has never been up north. "You'd love it," I tell him, and I never stop talking until he's heard about the empty fields around our trailer and the woods and the nearby swamp. "Even on sunny days, it's dark in the swamp. There are cypress trees and tamarack trees that turn gold this time of year, and there are bogs with weird plants, sundews and pitcher plants that eat insects. I've painted them a million times, and though you never see the animals that live in the swamp, you know they're there watching you."

I tell him about Mom and the fights with Dad and what a raw deal Mom got and how independent she is. I tell him how in the summer Mom had to work at the resort on the weekends because of all the tourists, so we had our Sunday on Monday. We'd sleep in and have a big breakfast and I'd squeeze fresh orange juice and Mom would make waffles. We'd sit outside and read the Sunday papers a day late, and then we'd go for a drive maybe to the sand dunes. We'd eat out, nothing fancy, just pizza or burgers, and when we got back home, we'd empty the sand out of our shoes and brush it from our hair. "I really miss those days, Thomas."

Thomas tells me about how his relatives are all supporting his med-school education. "We're all one big family," he says. "What's mine is yours, and what's yours is mine. That's the way Chaldeans are."

"What part of Iraq do Chaldeans come from?"

"Originally from Nineveh, Old Testament country. Remember Babylonia in the Bible? But my own ancestors hailed from a village in Iraq called Telkaif. No one's ever heard of it, but the Iraq War made nearby towns like Mosul and Kirkuk famous."

A freighter moves silently along the river, all its

lights on. It has a festive look, as if it's been lit with candles for a celebration. The violence of a war seems far away. I ask, "So you aren't Muslim."

"No. We speak Aramaic, the same language Jesus spoke. Dad can speak Arabic because he went to the Iraqi national school. My family is great, but I can't get away from them. I love that closeness, but it seems like they all have a piece of me. They have my life planned. Marry Mary. Be a doctor to Chaldean families. Help send for more relatives. I understand all that. But my life's like a book someone else has written, with no suspense, no need to turn the pages."

"What would you do if you could do whatever you want?"

"I don't know. One of my friends is heading for Haiti after he graduates. He's going to be working in a hospital for children with disabilities. Another guy is going to Alaska. He'll be a doctor, but he'll be spending a lot of time hunting and fishing too. I'm not saying I want to do stuff like that; I'm only saying I'd like to be able to make a choice."

"This is America. They can't make you do what you don't want to do."

"Maybe you noticed the car I'm driving. Over two hundred thousand miles. Bald tires, rust. When I take Mary out, Dad says, 'Take the new car, Thomas.' That's because he approves of my going out with Mary but not with anyone else. But I won't sneak around. When he asked where I was going tonight, I said I was showing you a little of Detroit."

"What did he say?"

Thomas looked uncomfortable. "He said, 'It's a disgrace that at her age her father lets her go out in public with a man.' I said, 'She's only a kid,' and Dad said, 'You must be blind.' And I guess I was."

Thomas puts his hand over mine and takes a nervous look around. He gives me an apologetic smile, "There are Chaldeans everywhere, and they're all related to me."

We head home. Both of us pull back a little

self-consciously with our confidences. I guess neither of us is used to talking about ourselves to someone we hardly know. As he drops me off, there's no "See you next week," just "Thanks for being a good listener" and "Say hello to your dad."

Everything is strangely quiet when I walk into the house. I'm drowned in streams of guilt. I shouldn't have left Dad. How has the elf child managed? I see the light under the studio door and open the door an inch at a time. Ruth is still sitting in the chair, a patient smile on her face. Dad swings around and in an accusing voice says, "Back so soon?"

I give a quick, fearful glance at the painting and gulp. A distorted chair takes up almost all of the canvas. It's huge. The slats on the chair back and arms look like the bars of a cell imprisoning Ruth, who sits poised and smiling. It's Ruth's innocence versus the overpowering world.

Dad waves Ruth off the chair. She hops down gracefully and goes over to look at the painting. I hold my breath. After she sees it, will she ever want to come back?

"You got me, all right," she says, "but you can't paint a chair. You should practice chairs."

Dad doesn't hear her. He's heading upstairs. I try to pay Ruth, but she won't accept money. Instead she hands me her notebook to mark the time she's leaving. "If I take money," she says, "the hours don't count. The one who gets the most hours is going to our convention in Chicago this winter." She turns over the pages so I can see all her good deeds carefully noted like in St. Peter's notebook at the pearly gates. I wonder what Dad would think if he knew he was a good deed.

I pick up my cell and call Mom to tell her about tonight. "You say he's in medical school? How did you meet him?"

I explain about the store.

"Oh, that's right. I was afraid you had met him in a hospital or something."

"No, everything's fine here." Under my breath I

add, *For the moment*, so it's not a complete lie. "They have a pathway along the river," I say. "We just sat there and talked."

"I'm glad you have a friend," Mom says, "but don't get too involved. You're there to go to school."

"Yes," I say.

9

*H*alloween comes and goes. We have our first November snow—city snow, gray and sloppy. We fall into a routine. Dad has a midget breakfast of toast and peanut butter, then disappears into his studio with a mug of coffee. Some days he paints for hours; other days it's quiet in the studio and, when I bring in lunch, I find Dad stretched out on the sofa asleep. But Ian Morgan's in ecstasy. He can't say enough good things about the paintings. We've crated and shipped four more. I can build a crate by myself now.

Morgan calls, and he and Dad talk about lighting

and space. I learn that in hanging pictures, the space between the paintings is almost like its own painting, and you have to think about that too. Dad gets emails from Morgan telling him how he has lined up this critic and that one to be at the opening. He's assuming Dad will be there, but I know he won't be strong enough. Even going up the stairs is too much for him now, so I've made up the couch in the studio as a bed. The old sofa with its worn upholstery and sagging springs has taken on a new importance, done up in white sheets and a pink blanket. Dad shrugs off not being at the opening. "My absence will create a stir, a nice bit of gossip. That's good for business. The critics can make up stories about me. They love stories."

Sometimes Dad still flies into a rage. "Go home!" he screams at me. "I can't work with you here. You're nothing but a leech. All you're interested in is what you can get out of me, living in my house, eating my food, watching me paint so you can steal my technique." He slams the door of the studio, and I hear him inside muttering. I know when he yells that he's having trouble with one of his paintings and someone has to be blamed, but it's so unfair. I want to storm into the studio and remind Dad about all I'm giving up to take care of him. But I have to admit that a lot of what he says is true. I am living in his house and eating his food, and when he's in the mood, he does teach me. And that's so amazing. One day I learn about glazes, how one thin translucent layer of paint laid over another and another can build a depth of color. I learn to avoid fussiness. Every detail is there because it's building the story of the painting. If it's not necessary, you have to get rid of it. You have to be ruthless. I learn composition and how to make people look at what you want them to look at in a painting. How powerful is that!

I take everything I learn and apply it to my own work. I've driven back to Belle Isle often for inspiration. The weather is cold now, and I seldom see anyone there. It's like the whole island has been picked up and shaken until it's empty of everything but the geese. The leafless trees, the bare willow tendrils blowing in the wind, the deserted beaches, and the picnic table with a cloth of snow. I take all the emptiness home and paint it, stealing everything I've learned from Dad.

I long to show him my work, but after the last time I'm terrified that he'll tell me again how bad it is and that I'll lose faith in what I'm doing.

The worst days are when Dad has an appointment with the doctor. He makes excuses. He's not well enough to go, or he's got to finish a painting while the idea is still clear in his head, or the doctor is a fool and doesn't know anything. Dad slams doors, refuses to dress; and when we finally get to the doctor's office, he won't answer the doctor's questions. Luckily Dr. Aziz is an older man and he's seen it all, so Dad's churlishness doesn't faze him. Somehow he's learned that Dad is a well-known artist. I'm sure it's from Thomas. They must have talked when Dad was in the hospital. The doctor puts up with Dad, humors him, and treats him like he's something between a mad genius and a spoiled child.

The trip we made to the doctor today has exhausted

Dad. When we get home, he lies down and I know he'll sleep the rest of the afternoon. I need Lila's cheeriness. It's been weeks since I've seen her.

"Come on over, girl. I've got a surprise for you."

When I pull up in front of her aunt's house, I see that next to the alterations notice there's a new sign: LILA'S ATELIER. Aunt Ernestine is busy at work, but she looks up when I walk in. "Kate, honey, how are you doing? How's that grandpa of yours?"

Before I can answer, Lila grabs me and pulls me into the dining room, only it isn't a dining room anymore. She's got skirts and blouses displayed, some on racks, some hanging by hooks on the walls. They're all a swirl of prints and bright colors. It's an exotic bazaar. A couple of girls are behind a screen, giggling and trying on clothes.

"It's fantastic," I tell her.

"I've been designing like crazy, and my auntie's been working nonstop making everything. Someone at school made a flyer for me for her class project, and I've got them everywhere. I even have a website, and someone from the local newspaper is coming to do a story. I wanted to quit school and do this full-time, but Auntie says she'll kick me out if I quit. Anyhow, school's not so bad. I made friends with this girl who does the coolest jewelry with African beads a friend of hers in the Peace Corps sends her, and I promised her she could sell it here." She lowers her voice. "I met this supercool fellow, J.K., who is learning to design cars. He's already won a prize. You should see his clay model. It's not all clunky like most cars. He says he wants it to look like it was shaped by the wind."

Lila's aunt calls in to us, "Don't think I don't know why you're whispering, Lila. Boys. You came down here to go to school, and that's what you're going to do, or I'll send you right back to Flint, and there's no plane that flies from Flint to Paris like there is in Detroit, girl."

I unwrap a painting of Belle Isle I've brought for Lila and her aunt. I blush as I give it to her. "I promised you a painting, but you don't have to hang it up or anything."

Lila is quiet for a minute and I don't breathe. Then she pokes me and says, "I knew you could paint, but you're good. You are *real* good."

I'm happy. I know Lila isn't the kind to just tell you what you want to hear. Yet in spite of her praise something hurts. I complain, "Look at you. You've got everything: school and your own shop with people actually buying your creations. I'm not going to school, and no one sees my paintings. They're just sitting there gathering dust."

"So why don't you try to sell some paintings?"

"Where would I sell them, and who would want to buy them?"

"Some of the kids at school have a co-op gallery with art students from Wayne State. It's just a hole in the wall, but they sell stuff. Some of the regular galleries even go down there and take things. Give it a try."

I'm afraid of being judged. Dad said my work was no good. If the gallery says the same thing, I'll lose heart. I don't know.

★ ★ ★

Somehow I get my nerve and the next afternoon I call Ruth, sign her book, and take two of the Belle Isle paintings that I've framed with cheap metal frames to the Tergiversate Gallery. Crazy name. I looked up the word in the dictionary and it said "to repeatedly change your opinion," so I'm hoping the gallery is open to all kinds of art.

I have a hard time finding the gallery, which is hidden between a cleaner's and an all-night drugstore. The gallery is in what looks like an abandoned store. The windows, with big bites missing from the glass, are boarded up so you can't see inside, but the boards have been painted with squares of bright color and there is a sign: TERGIVERSATE GALLERY.

A guy and a girl about a year or two older than I am are hanging pictures. Landscapes, portraits, explosions of colors, abstracts, color field, superrealism, even some images that aren't painted at all, just projected onto the wall. Everything is here. The boy gives me a quick over-the-shoulder glance. He's thin and pale, with long black hair and one of those funny little beard things beneath his lower lip. "No more! No more!" he shouts. "Take them away!" I hurry toward the door.

"Shut up, Pearce," the girl says. "Let's see what you've brought. But I warn you, he's right. We're loaded."

I fight the impulse to walk out of the gallery before someone tells me my work is no good. Pearce comes over and wrests my paintings from me. "Don't be modest," he says.

He looks at them a long time, and I'm shriveling. "Europe?" he asks. "You've been traveling?"

The girl, who has a long blond braid snaking down to her waist, is curious. She walks over and gives the paintings a long look and says, "It's Belle Isle, stupid."

Pearce looks angry at his mistake. "Of course. I should have known."

"I like them," the girl says. "They're in."

Before I can take a breath, Pearce says, "I'm not sure, Diane." He's still embarrassed about not recognizing the island, but Diane is already walking around the gallery holding the paintings, looking for a place to hang them.

She tells me, "You've captured the island and something more. It doesn't look like just Belle Isle. What you've done is make it look like all the lonely places in the world."

Pearce doesn't say anything, but he takes down a huge painting of a rat and helps Diane hang my two paintings in the newly emptied space. We all stand back and look at them as if we're art critics from the *New York Times*. I'm thrilled, but at the same time I'm desperate to get the paintings back, terrified at having them out of my hands and exposed for all the world to see. There are things in the paintings that I have a sudden urge to make better.

Pearce offers me a pop, and Diane says, "If you're not doing anything, you can help us hang the show. We're running short on time."

"There aren't any bosses or committees here," Pearce says. "Everybody works, and everybody has a say."

"What he means is it's chaos," Diane says. "Screaming arguments, late nights, hurt feelings, but this is our second year."

Five minutes later I'm up a ladder with a hammer. For a while I just do as I'm told, but when they tell me to hang two paintings side by side that fight with each other, I object. After a minute Diane says, "Right, split them up."

We call for pizza and work until everything is on the walls. Then we stand there pleased with our work. In our eyes the shabby, chilly gallery is the Metropolitan Museum of Art and the Louvre all rolled into one.

"Opening's Thursday night," Pearce says. "Bring a friend."

I hurry home, worried about Dad and Ruth. I didn't expect to be so late. When I get there, Dad is sitting at the kitchen table, lapping up a bowl of tomato soup that Ruth has heated. She has buttered a little stack of crackers for him, which sits next to the soup bowl. Dad gives me a smart-alecky wink that says, *Who needs you?*

Ruth whispers to me, "He wasn't going to eat, but I told him we get extra points for preparing and serving a dinner to an elderly person, so he said he would."

Aloud she tells me, "I'd stay and do the dishes, but I've got homework."

I sign Ruth's book, give her a hug, and run her home. When I get back, I find Dad in his studio. The painting of Ruth in the enormous chair is amazing. She appears wonderfully poised and smiling while all around her is this outsize, frightening world of giant chairs and tables and the enormous overpowering room.

"Where were you this afternoon?" Dad asks. "You're supposed to be here taking care of me, not wandering all over the city."

"Ruth seems to do a better job than I do." I'm pleased that Dad has even noticed my not being there.

"That's because she minds her own business," Dad says. "I need her back to finish the painting."

"She's coming Thursday night."

"Where are you going?"

"I thought we were minding our own business." Then I tell Dad all about the gallery opening. "They took two of my paintings."

The affable, mild man disappears and there is Frankenstein's monster. "A gallery opening. Just an opportunity for people who want to be seen. You'll cheapen your work by putting it in a fly-by-night gallery. You're not ready to show yet anyway. You're nothing but an amateur, a Sunday painter. You can't paint until you know something about life. That little child who comes here playing at taking care of me knows more about life than you do. Did you know her father deserted the family, and her mother has to work and leave that child alone?"

Furious, I scream at him, "Sounds just like the story of my own life!"

He turns pale and starts to gulp for air like a goldfish thrown out of a bowl. He sinks down on the couch, gasping. Frightened I go to him, but he waves me away. I dial 911. I live a dozen lifetimes until the ambulance comes, the siren on, the red lights pulsing. In seconds the medical-emergency team is taking off Dad's shirt. They bring in some kind of contraption, a defibrillator, one of them tells me. They get a stretcher

and strap Dad onto it and wheel him out the door.
What have I done?

I lock the house and drive to Receiving Hospital.
I search the emergency room, but Dad's already been
taken to urgent care. Two hours pass. I keep hoping
Thomas will come and tell me Dad's okay, just more
fluid in his lungs. They'll get rid of it, and he'll be fine.

A doctor, not Thomas, tells me Dad has had a coro-
nary incident, and they have admitted him to intensive
care. He says I should go home and come back tomorrow. There's nothing I can do. With a terrible pang
of guilt I tell myself he's right—I have already done
it. I sit in the waiting room another hour, wanting to
be close to Dad, but when the nurse gives me a worried look, I leave. The Red Wings hockey game is
just over, and the expressway is full of cheering fans
on their way home. The cheering seems unfair. Don't
they know about Dad?

Tonight when I call Mom, I'm in a reminiscent
mood, looking to escape from my worry about Dad
to another time and another place. "Do you remember

when I was little and you took me to Lake Michigan for a picnic and you went swimming far out in the lake and I started crying because I thought you would drown?"

Mom knows me inside and out. Right away she says, "Kate, you sound funny. What's the matter? Do you want me to come down there? I have a couple of days of vacation coming and it's the slow season at the resort."

Now I'm making Mom worry. "No, I'm fine." I don't want Mom telling me to come home or, *worse*, coming down here herself. I search for an explanation for the way I must sound. "Well there *is* something," I tell her. "I had two paintings accepted by a gallery. The show opens Thursday night, and they're already up on the gallery wall."

"That's terrific, honey. Can you get someone to take a picture for me to see?" There's a pause. "I suppose he's pleased."

"Oh, you know Dad. He's cool about it."

Somehow I get through the rest of the conversation,

answering questions and asking a few of my own, but as the call goes on, I'm afraid I'll lose control and scream, "Help!" At last I sign off.

I think of November up north. It's deer season. The deer pole will be up in our little village, the gutted deer hanging in a row as the hunters show off their trophies. Before daylight I'd have been in the woods behind our trailer, stamping out the tracks in the snow so the hunters wouldn't be able to find our deer.

When I awaken to the cheerless Detroit daylight, I dial the hospital. Dad has had an uneventful night. How can that be? How can a night when you're taken by ambulance to the hospital and you're in intensive care be uneventful?

I shower, gulp down some coffee, and take off. There are strict visiting hours for intensive care, and I have to wait. I sit with other unhappy and frightened folks in a lounge where coffee is available. There's a stack of magazines that must reflect the taste of the people on the hospital staff: golf, parenting, decorating magazines. I read them cover to cover and remember nothing. When I read one over again, everything is brand-new.

At last we're allowed into intensive care, where the patients' beds are gathered around the nurses' station like kindergartners around a favorite teacher. I find Dad, who gives me a cross look as if this is all my fault, and I know it is. He has an IV going, but the frightening paleness is gone.

"I want to get out of here."

"We have to talk with the doctor."

"That boy doctor from the convenience store was here."

"Thomas."

A staff doctor appears. He's probably already seen a dozen patients by now, so he's skipping the bedside manner, giving all his attention to the heart monitor over Dad's bed. He fools around with his stethoscope. "How are we doing?" he finally asks, as if there are several people in Dad's bed. Or maybe I'm included in his question.

"I want to be released," Dad says. In a threatening voice he adds, "You can't keep me if I want to go."

"Oh, no," the doctor says, and sizes Dad up. "We can release you right away. If this is your daughter here, she can alert the funeral home so there's no time wasted."

Dad shuts up. The doctor has won, and now he's the gracious host. "Actually you're doing very well. We just want to make you comfortable and take a look at what's going on. You'll be on your way home in a day or two, after we've adjusted your medication and gotten rid of the fluid that's accumulating in your lungs and putting stress on your heart." He makes a few notes on the chart and moves on.

"What did he write?" Dad asks.

I look, but it's all scribbles and weird medical talk.

As I leave, Dad says, "Not a word to Morgan."

In the corridor I see Thomas. In a flood of tears I pour out my story. "I'm sure it's what I said that did it."

Thomas leads me to an out-of-the-way corner and puts a consoling arm around my shoulders, but his words are not gentle. "You're making yourself too important. Guilt comes from feeling we're at the center of the universe. We're not. We're just a small part of someone's life; there are a hundred thousand other things going on. In the case of your father it's his cirrhosis, exacerbated by portal hypertension."

When I look puzzled, he says, "Don't worry about the medical terms, but I'm afraid, Kate, you have to face the fact that there will be more of these episodes."

Why is it we only have to face bad things? No one ever says, *I'm afraid, Kate, you have to face the fact that your father is just fine or that you'll be a famous artist.* I ask, "How long does Dad have?"

"You can never tell, but I'd guess months. They're going to keep your dad in for a few days and release him on Friday. That'll give you a little rest. I haven't seen you around. What are you up to?"

I tell him about the gallery and my two paintings. "No one's going to buy them, but I love seeing them on the wall."

"Fantastic. I'll be able to say I knew you when."

I blurt out, "The opening's tomorrow night. I can bring a friend."

"Could I be the friend? I'm off duty."

So it's all arranged. I drive home and walk into the empty house. Not my fault, Thomas said, but I don't know. I try to concentrate on the opening tomorrow night. What will it be like to walk into the gallery and maybe hear someone talking about my paintings? What if they say something soul shriveling? Or what if everyone just ignores them? Suddenly I'm not sure I want to be there; only now that I've asked Thomas to come, it's too late to back out. I open the door to the studio and Dad's paintings scold me. They tell me all that's important is doing everything I can to help Dad get ready for his show. This is his last opportunity, his last chance. "Months," Thomas said. I have years ahead of me. I can wait. I look at the painting of the little girl lost in the big chair and suddenly it's me.

10

I'm at the hospital for the morning visiting hours. Dad is out of the ICU and in a regular room. I tell Dad how great the painting of Ruth is and ask if it's finished.

"Of course it's finished. Can't you tell? I thought you pretended to be an artist. I want to get home and send it off." He growls about having to spend another night in the hospital. In a loud voice he complains about the food and the nurses and about the man in the bed next to him who keeps the TV on. I try to hush Dad and look apologetically at Dad's roommate, but he's totally involved in a soap opera.

Back home I get out wood, saw, hammer, and nails. It takes all day, but the crate is finally finished and ready for Dad. Just as I try the painting in the crate to be sure of the fit, I make a tiny scratch on the surface of Ruth's blue dress.

I'm destroyed. Dad's a perfectionist. He'll see the scratch. I mix cerulean blue with a touch of white. My hand is shaking. The brush barely touches the canvas. The match is perfect. I'm sure he won't notice. I can't help grinning. I'll have a part in Dad's show. Maybe a famous museum will buy Dad's painting of Ruth, and I'll stand in front of the painting and know there's a tiny bit of my own work on the canvas.

There's just time for a shower and a blow-dry before the opening. There's a spot on my blouse, and rubbing it with water makes it worse. The doorbell. Too late to change. Thomas takes my arm and heads for the car. It's not the old jalopy but the Lincoln, and there is a girl in the front seat. He's going to leave me at the opening and take off with his girlfriend.

"This is Mary." He says my name to her. She gives me a big smile. Well, why wouldn't she? She's got the guy. She is drop-dead gorgeous, with long black hair and black eyes.

Thomas opens the rear door, and I slide in like Cinderella getting into the wrong coach.

"I hope you don't mind," Mary says with an accent that sounds French but probably isn't. "Since you're going by the university, I asked Thomas if he would drop me off."

I can breathe again. "No, of course I don't mind. It's nice to meet you."

Thomas says, "The good news is that when Dad heard I was going out with Mary, he gave me the keys to this baby instead of the crate."

Mary is busy with her cell, and when we pull up in front of one of the university buildings, a young man hurries over to the car and helps Mary out. They walk away arm in arm.

Thomas motions me up front. "Like Mary, Mark is here on a student visa. My dad's not too happy about

Mary dating him." He smiles at me. "But let's forget about all that and have a little fun. I've never been to a gallery opening. Should I have a beard and a beret?"

The gallery is crowded and about a hundred degrees. It's mostly students, and I recognize a couple of kids from the art school. Thomas looks at a wacky sculpture made of burned candles molded into a contorted shape. "The guy's kidding, right?" he asks.

I push my way over to the wall where we hung my paintings, and there they are. One has a red dot on the card with my name and the painting's title. "It's sold!" I screech. Not very cool, but I can't help it.

Thomas jokes, "I ought to get a commission for taking you to the island."

I feel a hand on my shoulder. It's Lila.

We hug, and she says, "Your pictures are terrific, girl, but your clothes are shabby. Didn't I teach you anything? You take the money from your sale and come shop at my place."

I introduce Thomas, and Lila sizes him up. "Are you the doctor looking after Kate's granddad?"

Thomas is about to correct her when I interrupt. "Thomas is a sophomore in medical school, but he explains all the medical words to me and he keeps an eye on my grandfather for me." Thomas gives me a quick look at the word *grandfather* but keeps quiet.

We push our way through the crowd and circle the gallery. Lila and I explain the art to Thomas, who appears to know nothing except what he dislikes.

"Most of the stuff is weird."

"You have to study it, experience it," I tell him. "It's no different from studying medicine."

"Medicine is a science. Art is supposed to be accessible."

"Yes, but not easy," I tell him.

Diane comes over to us, and *surprise*, she knows Thomas. He looks embarrassed.

"Hi," Diane says to him. "You can't have the painting until the show is over."

Lila and I stare at Thomas. His face is red, and he doesn't know where to look.

Diane puts her hand over her mouth. "Did I give something away?"

I'm destroyed. I was imagining that a distinguished art collector had wandered into the gallery and, bypassing all the other art, lasered onto my painting. Or maybe it was a curator from the Detroit Institute of the Arts, wanting it for the museum's permanent collection. But no. It's Thomas, who doesn't know anything about art, who bought my painting. I try to calm down. Here is this great guy who made his way to this obscure gallery and paid money he couldn't afford just to make me happy.

I give him a hug and tell him he's the nicest person in the world.

He's protesting. "I didn't buy it. I mean I bought it, but I bought it for someone else."

"Right," I say. "You're just an agent for the Museum of Modern Art. I really appreciate your buying the painting, but it's going to be a gift. I can't possibly take your money."

"I'm trying to tell you it's not my money."

He's so insistent, I have to believe him. Who else knew about the show? I look at Lila.

"Not my money, honey. That's a great painting, but all my money goes into the shop."

No one else knew, except for Mom, and she's hundreds of miles away. Wait. Dad knew. "It was my dad."

Thomas says, "He'll kill me if he finds out you know."

Right in front of everyone I dissolve in a flood of tears, and my friends all crowd around me in a kumbaya moment. They get me some Coke to drink and ply me with cheese and crackers. I pull myself together and tell Lila I'll explain later. The gallery is filling up. They're playing a k. d. lang song about life being sad and dull, but beautiful. And it is. No one's looking at the paintings. They're all talking. I think of how Dad said people go to openings just to be seen, but I love being part of this. It's exciting. Thomas hits it off with Pearce, who like Thomas is a big Tigers fan.

He shows us one of his own paintings of the old

Tiger stadium, with ghostly fans sitting in ghostly bleachers. The long shadows of the fans are lost in darkness while the players are all in a blaze of lights. Thomas has found a picture he loves. He looks longingly at the painting, checks the price, and gives a big sigh.

"Tell you what," Pearce says. "Next time I need an operation, we'll trade."

Diane comes up to me. "We sold your other painting. The woman who bought it wants to meet you."

She's much older than most of the people in the gallery, mousy-looking with a long skirt and a sloppy sweater in a drab shade. I'm disappointed. It's not the way I pictured the owner of my work.

"I love your painting," she says. "I've never bought any art before. I stopped in because I work at the cleaner's next door. Then I saw your painting of Belle Isle. When I was growing up, my mom and dad used to take me there. They had pony rides and an elephant house and we'd pack our dinner and have it at a picnic table on the water, just like the one you painted. We'd stay and watch the freighters at night, just like you've got it lit up in your painting. I can't tell you how it takes me back. It's like we're all together again." She grabs my hand and gives it a squeeze. "I didn't mean to take up your time. I just wanted to tell you."

She hurries away. So no collector to slap one more painting on his wall. No curator to shove my painting down in the storeroom of the museum with its other second-best stuff. Instead my painting has found the perfect owner, someone to look at it hundreds of times a day, to live in my painting, to love it for giving her back a piece of her past. I've only been thinking of what the painting has meant to me, forgetting that once it's sold, it's part of someone else's life and just as important to them as it is to me. Maybe I'll talk to Dad about that.

On the way home I promise Thomas I won't tell Dad that I know who bought the painting. After I say good-bye to Thomas, I call Justin on my cell. I have to tell someone about selling my paintings.

He congratulates me and then asks, "How much did you get?"

In a second he's multiplied the amount by three hundred and sixty-five. "If you do two pictures a day, every day for a year, you'll have fifty-four thousand, seven hundred and fifty dollars."

"It's not like making doughnuts or building birdhouses," I tell him. "You have to be inspired, and it takes days and sometimes years to get a painting the way you want it."

"Well, what you're doing is working," he says. "So congratulations. We've got our own art right here on Lake Superior. Slices of ice are starting to pile up along the shore."

After we say good-bye, I imagine this winter's icy towers and think what a great painting that would make.

When Dad is finally released from the hospital, he's his usual complaining self. "Why weren't you there to pick me up earlier?" "Why all the forms to fill out?"

"It's a prison." He's not interested in the instructions for his medication. "Doctors don't know anything." At last he's transferred from the wheelchair to the car and we take off.

I tell him about the opening. "And the most exciting thing is that I sold both of my paintings." I tell him about the woman and her memories of Belle Isle. "I don't know who bought the other painting," I say, "but I could have died with happiness."

"Whoever it was," he says, "if they're shopping in that gallery, you can be sure they don't know a thing about art."

Silence from me.

Dad gives me a rare glance of approval when he sees how I've built the crate for his painting of Ruth. I hold my breath, worried that, perfectionist that he is, he may detect the scratch I repaired, but no, it's okay. Although he can hardly totter over to his easel, he works on his last painting. It looks finished to me. It's a painting of enormous cars on an expressway that stretches out forever. His paintings have giant autos, huge computers, and big furniture, everything absorbing and overcoming, swallowing up midget people. He fusses, painting and then painting out what he's done. I think he doesn't want to finish this work because then what? Everything is a terrible effort. Clearly he isn't strong enough to begin another work. Painting has been his whole life, and now he'll never paint again.

A frantic call from Morgan makes him let go, and together we build the last crate. The UPS man, who is an old friend by now, carts the final painting away.

Dad is in a rare good mood, so I dare to ask, "What makes artists want to keep painting?"

He gives me a disgusted look. "If you have to ask that question, you have no business being an artist."

"I know about wanting to paint," I say, and although it feels disloyal, I tell him about the fights I had with Mom about my painting. "But I don't mean just *wanting* to paint. What I mean is that a lot of artists never get famous like you have, no one ever sees their work, but they keep painting."

Dad says, "No one else can paint the picture you

are painting, and if you don't paint it, that glimpse of the world that you had will be lost. All those years I wasted, I lost so much, and—I don't care how immodest it sounds—the world lost as well."

He points to the door and turns his back on me. I hurry upstairs to my own little studio. The world's not losing any of my ideas.

We get endless emails now from Morgan. He can't say enough good things about the coming exhibition. He's invited the curators from the Whitney and the Museum of Modern Art to have what he calls "a peek" at the paintings. "They'll both want the same ones. There'll be a bidding war; more money than you've ever dreamed of, Quinn. I've got buyers from Dubai, Russia, Hong Kong." He's not finished. He can't help writing, "When I see what you're capable of, I'm furious at how you've wasted your life." Then he adds, "The only good thing is you're still a young man. Your best years are ahead of you." I tell Dad what Morgan said, leaving out the last sentence.

11

The studio, empty of all its paintings and with nothing new started, has a deserted, eerie look.

Erlita and Dad have an argument. "Let me order you a regular hospital bed, Mr. Quinn. You've got plenty of room in here, and you'll be that much more comfortable. Plus I can't give you a proper washing on that sofa."

Dad won't have it. When I agree with her, Erlita orders it anyway. A man comes to set it up. It dominates the room like Dad's paintings used to. I learn how to move the head and foot up and down and how the rails work. Dad calls it a metal coffin and swears at the deliveryman, who hurries away.

Dad continues to sleep on the sofa. When he has trouble making it to the bathroom, Erlita tells me to get a portable potty, and I do. The studio has become a hospital room. After my one attempt at helping Dad shave, Dad decided to grow a beard, and now he looks like van Gogh.

One morning I bring in his breakfast to find him sleeping on the metal coffin. I should be relieved, but instead I'm sad. We push buttons and make a game of all the things the bed can do. I buy a small TV for the studio, and we watch old movies. Thomas calls a couple of times, but he hasn't called lately.

Erlita comes twice a week now. She tells me about a monitor I can get so I can hear Dad when I'm in my room or in my studio.

Lila calls me on her cell one afternoon when Erlita is there and says, "You've got to come over to the school right now. They've flooded the courtyard and it's a skating rink. I know someone who'll lend you skates."

I'm explaining why I can't go when Erlita interrupts me to say, "You need to get out. I'm finished for the day. I'll stay with your daddy for a couple of hours. Now go."

I tell Lila I'll be there, and I grab my coat. I'm used to the expressways now, so it takes me only minutes to get to the school, and sure enough, the kids are all gliding around the outdoor sculptures on their skates. I find Lila and put on the skates she's borrowed for me. Everyone is acting as if they're ten years old. We play crack the whip and we make a samba line. A boy I remember from one of my classes puts an arm around my waist, and we join hands and skate like we're in the ice-skating follies. A light snow drifts down on us, and we laugh at the way it lands on our eyelashes and gets into our mouths when we talk.

"Where have you been? I haven't seen you around," the boy says.

"I had to drop out this semester," I say. "I'll be back though."

"What's your cell number?" he asks, and takes off

his glove to write it down. His name is Adam. Lila skates by and gives me a thumbs-up. The winter sun disappears, and the cars on the busy street turn on their headlights. I have to get home. I say good-bye to Adam and Lila and hurry away. What I said to Adam is true. I promise myself I *will* come back to the school.

When I hurry into the house, Erlita grins at me. "Look at those rosy cheeks. Don't you stay holed up here in this house. You talk your daddy into getting someone in on a regular basis so you can get out."

Before I can do that, Dad has a bad day and I take him to the hospital, where they admit him for a couple of days. I don't want to sit by myself in the empty house, so I drive around the city looking for something to take my mind off Dad's illness. I guess I have death in the back of my mind, because when I see an ancient cemetery in the middle of the city, I drive in. The marble angels wear coats of snow. There are big, old trees and a few containers with flowers that have wilted in the cold wind. I recognize the names of old Detroit families on the tombstones: Brush, Canfield,

Cass. They're street names now. The cemetery is not sad. It's restful, as if death were a nap you steal in the middle of the afternoon.

On the way home I stop at the convenience store to pick up some milk, and I see Thomas and Mary getting into the Lincoln. I wave, and they pause to wait for me. Thomas must be taking Mary to see her boyfriend. Maybe he and I can do something after. I'd love to get out of the house.

"Dad's in the hospital, so I've got the night off," I tell Thomas, and look expectantly at him.

Thomas says, "Mary and I are heading off to a concert." He names a famous rock band. "I'd invite you to come along," he says, "but it's sold out."

"Thanks. I promised Lila I'd stop by anyhow." I say good-bye and hurry into the store. Emmanuel is behind the counter. He has been less than friendly with me lately, but tonight he's all smiles. "You saw Thomas and Mary?" he asks. "They're going to hear some music. They played me a CD and I put my hands over my ears. They make a nice couple, yes?"

He gives me a sympathetic look. "You're too thin. I'm throwing in a box of Christmas cookies. No charge."

I drive over to see Lila, who's getting ready to go home to Flint for Christmas. On the way I console myself by eating the whole box of cookies.

Lila asks, "Is your mama coming down to have Christmas with you and your granddaddy?"

I'm choking with the truth and I have to tell someone. "Can I swear you to secrecy?" I ask.

"I'm the best at keeping secrets."

"My grandfather is my father."

"What are you talking about!"

So I tell her.

"Dalton Quinn is your daddy? You're making this up, right?"

"No." I show her the car registration with Dad's name.

"I heard he came back to Detroit. But you've got a different name."

"That's because of how Mom feels."

"So how sick is he?"

"The doctor says he only has months." I can't keep the quiver out of my voice.

Lila puts an arm around me. "You can't say anything to your mama?"

"No. She would come and take me home, and I have to help Dad get ready for the show. It's critical that the gallery doesn't know how sick Dad is. They're counting on having more of his work."

"You mean he's a kind of investment?"

"To them, yes. But for Dad it's his last chance to get some recognition for his work."

"Is there anything I can do for you?"

"No. Just telling someone has helped a lot." And it has.

Aunt Ernestine makes me stay for dinner. She and Lila keep pushing food at me like I'm one of those geese you force to eat so its liver gets bigger and tastier. Lila asks me what I'm working on, and I tell her

I haven't had the heart to pick up a brush lately. "I guess I figure if Dad can't paint anymore, it's not fair for me to."

"That's the dumbest thing I ever heard," Lila says. "You're just punishing yourself, girl."

I tell Lila's aunt about Dad, and she says, "That's all the more reason for you to keep at your painting. Your daddy is going to feel a whole lot better if he knows you're following in his footsteps."

I think about what she says. She has a point, but Dad was never a big one for appreciating someone else's work. Besides, how could I ever follow in his footsteps? Then I ask myself why I should always measure my work against his. Didn't Dad say no one else could paint the picture that you do, and if you don't paint it, your glimpse of the world is gone forever? Suddenly my fingers are itching to pick up a brush and put down what I saw, and especially what I felt, in the cemetery. I get up from the table and say I have to get home. Aunt Ernestine gives me some brownies for the road, and Lila gives me a scarf with colors that haven't even been invented. I give them both hugs and hurry back to my painting.

Mom calls that night. She wants me home for Christmas. "School's out, isn't it?"

"Yes, but there's going to be a student show on the first of the year and I have to finish a couple of paintings I want to submit." I hate making up an excuse, but I can't leave Dad.

Silence. "I could come down there, stay at a motel. Your dad wouldn't have to know I'm in town. You and I could go somewhere for a nice Christmas dinner. They've hired me permanently for the manager's job, and I'm making good money."

For a minute it seems possible, and there's nothing in the world I want more than to be with Mom for Christmas, but how could I explain having to leave her alone to take care of Dad? I almost break down and tell Mom the truth, but I know she'd want to take me home, and Dad needs me. "I'd better just concentrate on the painting," I tell her.

"Sure," she says, "I understand." But I can tell by

her voice that she doesn't.

I stay up most of the night making a small painting of the pine tree in our yard in Larch that we always decorated for the birds at Christmastime with strings of dried cherries and cranberries, and ornaments made of peanut butter and melted fat. Underneath the tree we left corn for the squirrels and raccoons. I paint our trailer in the background, with lit windows and the outline of the two of us in one of them. In the morning I mail it to Mom, and then I go to pick up Dad.

Thomas is waiting for me outside Dad's room. "The doctor wants to talk with you, Kate. I'll let him know you're here."

"How was the concert?"

"Fine. Look, I owe you an explanation."

"No. I mean what you do is your business."

"Kate, I know what my family went through to get here, and Mary's family is living in Lebanon practically starving." Thomas's voice is breaking. "It sounds dramatic, but the truth is if we get married, we'll have a better chance of bringing some of them over and maybe saving their lives. With us family is everything. Mary and I like each other. We'll be all right. It's a small sacrifice."

I understand sacrifice, giving up something you want for something more important. I just hope there isn't going to be a whole lot more of that in my life.

Evidently there is. Dad's doctor appears, looking incredibly businesslike. "Thomas here tells me you're taking care of your father by yourself. Have you considered a nursing home for him? I must be honest with you. The news is not good."

"Dad would hate a nursing home," I say. "We'll manage."

"He'll require full-time care. Even so it will be downhill. You're too young to do this on your own. I'd advise getting in nursing help."

I know the doctor is right, because this time Dad doesn't object to the wheelchair, and the minute we walk into the house, he heads for his bed. Something's changed.

Dad talks about starting a new painting, but it's too

much effort for him. "Not today," he says in a voice that has become a hoarse whisper.

I set up a small canvas on the tray table I use for his meals. It has a rack to hold books and newspapers, and I prop the canvas on that. Dad is pleased at first, and he makes a few swipes at the canvas with a brush. There are a string of curses.

"Gone," he says, and knocks the canvas to the floor. "What do you think you're doing to me?" he asks. His face is red and his breathing comes in heaves. "You want to see me make a fool of myself? It's payback time, isn't it? Getting back at me for deserting you. Well, what do you think my career would have been if I had stayed with you and your mother? Nothing. I'd have been nothing."

I run out of the room. I try to excuse him. He's dying and he'll never paint again . . . but he means what he said. He wasn't sorry he left us. I think now that Mom was right. I should never have come. It's one thing to *imagine* how Dad feels, but I don't want to hear him say it. From the window I see the cat prowling in the snow. I open the back door softly and call, "Kitty, kitty," in my most beguiling voice. It runs away. Not even the cat has any time for me.

Adam calls to ask me out, but I explain I have to take care of my father, who is sick. I don't tell him who my father is. He says he's going home for the holidays and will call me when he gets back.

For the next few days Dad mostly sleeps while I struggle to hold off Morgan, who wants Dad in New York. I no longer have the excuse of Dad working to get his paintings ready for the show. Everything has been sent.

"He has a little cold," I tell Morgan.

"What are you doing for it? Are you giving him vitamin C? And there's that stuff you rub in your nose."

"I'm letting him get a lot of rest."

"I think you should get a doctor. The show's only a couple of weeks away. He needs to be here. I heard the *New York Times* is holding space in their Sunday paper for a review of the show. We'll sell out. I feel it. Your father is going to be a rich man."

When I tell Dad, he gives a bitter laugh. "You can buy me an expensive coffin."

Talk like that destroys me. I don't want to think about what's going to happen. I'm practically killing *myself* to keep him alive.

It's three days before Christmas. At the market I buy a small tree, a real one that's potted to plant afterward. I bruise the needles to get the piney scent on my hands. It smells like home. I put the tree in the studio and trim it with paper chains I've made from printing out Morgan's emails. I don't remember much about the holidays when Mom and Dad were together, except for one time when Dad cut us a Christmas tree in the woods. He maneuvered it into the house and got it set up in the stand before we noticed a wasp nest between the branches. I mention it to Dad. He looks surprised, as if he hadn't thought I would remember. I also remember a Christmas Eve when he didn't turn up until long after I was in bed. When he finally came home that night, there were angry voices. I don't mention this memory.

I want to make Dad a special Christmas dinner. Erlita told me they have fresh turkeys at the Eastern Market, so I go and get one. Up north there are lots of turkey farms. A few days before Thanksgiving and Christmas you can see the turkeys lining up behind the slaughterhouse to wait their turn. I'm hoping this turkey will be as fresh.

There's a big Christmas present from Morgan. It's a check for five hundred thousand dollars. I can't believe all those zeros. I have to read the check three times. The accompanying letter says, "Here is a little advance. I have competing bids from the Museum of Modern Art and the Whitney for two of your paintings. You can leave your exile there at once and rent a decent loft or studio here in civilization. You'll need a place to see the critics who'll want to interview you. There's a terrific photographer lined up to do a portrait for the show's catalog. I'll look for you next week, and be sure to bring your daughter along for the opening. You won't want her in the loft, but my secretary here has a place in New Jersey and she would look after Kate for a day or two."

"Dad," I say, "we've got to tell Morgan the truth. He's arranging all this stuff because he thinks you'll be there."

"He loves doing it. No need to disappoint him. Let him have his fun. I'll try to make a timely exit so my obituary gets in the *New York Times* just before the show opens. Terrific publicity."

"That's an awful thing to say." I'm shaken and feel my eyes burning, but Dad only laughs.

Dad has a lawyer, Mr. Krull, come over, and they talk behind closed doors. I can tell from the way Mr. Krull's voice goes up and down that he has a lot of questions about what Dad wants to do. After he leaves, Dad tells me Mr. Krull will deposit several thousand dollars in an account at the bank in both Dad's name and mine. Grocery money, he says, and tells me to use some of it to buy myself clothes. I don't buy any clothes, but I do splurge on a fancy Christmas cake from the Polish bakery.

On Christmas morning I run to the window, hoping the weatherman was wrong and that there is fresh snow. Instead it's a typical Detroit winter day, overcast, with leftover mushy snow on the ground in shades of Portland gray medium and Portland gray dark. I brave Dad's protests and get him dressed up in his best sport shirt. For a Christmas present I've painted a portrait of Dad, but I'm afraid to give it to him. I'm afraid he'll say how amateurish it is.

He tells me he has something for me and it's in the front closet. I find a big package all wrapped in Christmas paper. Erlita must have done it for him. He watches me unwrap it. It's his pallet and paint box. I throw my arms around him and kiss him on the cheek. It's the first time I've done that, and we're both embarrassed. Feeling bold, I run upstairs and get the portrait. His hands are shaking as he holds it, and he looks at it for a long time. "Not bad," he says.

At dinner, which Dad hardly eats in spite of how

tender the turkey is, I try to get him talking about his own Christmases as a boy. The thing about having your parents separated is that you lose half your family stories. I want to catch up. "What was it like when you were a kid?" I ask, meaning Christmas, but that isn't what he talks about.

"My mother used to call me her changeling," he says. "You know what a changeling is? A child who has been substituted for the real child. I didn't care about what my dad and my brother cared about, fooling around with cars, hunting and fishing, never missing a high school basketball game on Friday nights. I mean, I did all those things and I was even good at some of them, but I didn't enjoy them. I was the best marksman in the family, but I hated the killing. I hated seeing the gutted bodies of the deer strung up in town on opening day."

I want to tell him I do too, but he doesn't give me a chance. Once he starts, he doesn't want to stop.

"I married your mother because everyone else was getting married."

I stared at him. "That's why you married Mom?"

"I know how that sounds, and it wasn't the only reason. I loved your mother, and I tried to put the two parts of my life together. The normal guy and the artist. It just didn't work. I'm not proud of what happened to our marriage. I know I've hurt people, but that's the way I am. What I care about is my work."

All he cares about is his work? *That's the way I am.* That's his excuse for hurting Mom and me? I've never been able to express how I feel about Dad's paintings, but now in my anger and disappointment it all comes out. "You're like your paintings," I say. "They're like a slap in everyone's face. They shock you with their ugliness, but they don't give you anything back." I remember van Gogh's ugly painting of the poor man and woman, and how you felt not only the ugliness but pity too. "There's no pity in your paintings."

"Pity is for weaklings. If I'd been a bleeding heart, I'd never have been the painter I am. I know what you're asking: Did I miss seeing you growing up? Of course I did. Would I rather have been a good father than a great artist? The answer is no."

I scream at him, "Why couldn't you be both, and why do you have to tell me these things? Just shut up!"

When Mom calls later in the evening, I say, "I'm coming home."

12

The next day I call Erlita. "Honey, someone has to stay with your daddy twenty-four hours a day. That's three nurse's aides, and that's a lot of money. And then there's the weekend. That's extra. Maybe you should be thinking about a nursing home."

"Money's not a problem." I call Mr. Krull.

"There is certainly more than enough money for nursing help," he tells me. "Actually I think it's an excellent idea. I told your father when I was there the other day that I felt strongly that caring for him is too much responsibility for a young girl. I don't think he

realized how much of a burden it is for you. I pointed
out that it's only going to get more difficult."

I thought about how when I told Dad I was going
home, he just nodded and even looked a little relieved. I
was upset at his reaction. After all I'd done for him, after
I'd given up school, he was glad to get rid of me? But
after talking with Mr. Krull I wonder . . . His wanting
to get rid of me doesn't make a lot of sense. Was Dad
saying those heartless things to me on purpose? Did he
know it was the only way he could make me leave?

I stay the week, helping Dad get used to the new
arrangement. At first he resents having strangers care
for him and won't talk to the nurse's aides, but he can't
get out of bed and knows he needs them. I'm afraid
the aides will be intimidated by Dad's shouting and
his demands, but even the shyest of the three seems
used to abuse. Maybe they know that Dad isn't fighting them; he's fighting his illness and his death. They
just happen to be in the middle of the battle.

I go to the store to say good-bye to Emmanuel,
hoping Thomas will be there, but he isn't.

"He and Mary went to a movie," Emmanuel says. "I'll tell him you stopped by. Who's going to take care of your father now?"

It's more than a question, it's an accusation. In their community, where family is everything, it would be unthinkable to leave a father, never mind what kind of father he is. Are they right? I don't know.

Late at night my guilt gets the better of me, taking over my sleep. I prowl around the kitchen, getting a glass of milk and a peanut-butter-and-crackers fix. Anita, the night aide, is there having a cup of tea. She's tall and slim and bony, with a rounded cap of closely cut hair and large eyes with faint brownish purple circles underneath. Each night she brings a small framed picture of a little boy and sets it up in the kitchen. It's like she's saying, *I'm sitting here all night for you, son. This money is going to make a difference in your life.*

"Your dad's sleeping like a baby," she reassures me. "I expect you'll be anxious to get home to your mama. A man sick as your dad is a handful for a young girl like you."

I'm relieved to have a sympathetic ear. "I don't know if I should leave him, but he wants me to go, so what else can I do?"

"I can see your dad is a proud man. Nothing's as hard as having to depend on someone else. And maybe he doesn't want you to see him at the end."

I consider what Anita says, and it makes sense. Dad wants me to remember him as he was, still in charge. Maybe he's worried I'll love him less when he's weak and helpless. Perhaps I should stay, but that would take away his ability to manage his life, and I can't do that. It has to be what he wants and not what I want.

In the morning it's time for the last thing on my list before I leave: telling Morgan the truth. Morgan's emails and phone calls are coming thick and fast. Interviews are scheduled. The famous 92nd Street Y wants Dad to give a talk. Dad has said nothing, wanting to let the interest and publicity swell, waiting until the last possible moment.

Dad calls me into the studio and directs me to get Morgan on his cell. I see him listening to Morgan, to what is probably Morgan's insistence on wanting details of Dad's arrival. Finally Dad says, "I'm not coming to New York, not now or ever. I can't even get out of bed."

I can hear Morgan shouting. Dad waits impatiently and then says, "If you just shut up, what I'm trying to tell you is that I'm dying. No! I'm not drunk. I'm not crazy. Just a minute." He hands me his cell.

We figured this would be how Morgan would take it. "It's true," I say. "Dad has cirrhosis of the liver. He tried to get a liver transplant, but he also has something called dilated congestive cardiomyopathy." And then I say, "He's very sick." I choke up.

Maybe it was Dad's voice, which is not much more than a whisper, maybe it's my listing the medical names of the terrible things that are happening to Dad, or maybe it's the way I lose it at the end, but Morgan believes me.

"What am I supposed to do?" Morgan says. He pulls himself together. "That's terrible. I'm really sorry. What a lousy break. This show is going to put him back on the map. It could have changed his life." There is a pause; then he adds, "Of course as soon as people know there won't be any more paintings by Quinn, the prices are bound to go up."

I punch the End key. Immediately the phone rings again.

"Don't answer," Dad says. He wants to know what Morgan said.

"He said how sorry he was."

I take off for the Tergiversate. I'm leaving three of my paintings at the gallery. "Where are you going?" Diane asks.

"Up north."

"That's the end of the world."

"It's the best part of the world. I'll send more paintings down to convince you."

I go to see Lila next. She takes my hand and pulls

me up the stairway to show me a couple of empty rooms. "Auntie's rented the rooms, and this summer we're moving up there to live. All the downstairs is going to be her alterations and my shop. I've designed a blouse in a lot of fabrics and colors. It is so neat and it's selling."

When I tell her about Dad and how I'll be going home she says, "I feel so sorry for your father. It must be hard taking care of him, but I hate to see you go. Promise you'll come back to school."

"I'm going to try. I really want to, but right now I don't see how."

"You sound like an old lady. Girl, you're only eighteen. You've got a life ahead of you, not behind you. Anyhow you've got to come back and see my new place."

We hug and I promise. She sends me away with one of the blouses.

That evening Thomas comes over. "Dad told me you were leaving."

I tell him how Anita thinks Dad wants me to go because he doesn't want me to see him get sicker and sicker and die.

"Anita is probably right. I've never seen anyone as determined to control things as your dad."

"I can't leave him." I start to cry. Thomas's arms go around me, and I smell the wool of his sweater, something he uses on his hair, and just a whiff of hospital. I haven't really been able to cry, and now I can't stop. Thomas digs out a handful of crumpled Kleenex, but I have my own. The harsh kitchen lights shine on my red eyes and nose. I'm sure my face is all blotchy.

"I just wish I had your father's guts," Thomas says. "I wish I were as certain and as brave as he is about what to do with my life. What about you?"

"I don't know. I still want to paint, but it's so connected with Dad now. Before I can come back to school, I'll need to work awhile to get the money for a place to stay anyhow."

"I'll look for your paintings one of these days at the Art Institute." He gives me a hug and then he's gone.

★ ★ ★

I'm not taking the bus up north. Dad insists on my flying back. My suitcase and backpack and a couple of small canvases I've been working on are stacked at the door, waiting for the taxi that will take me to the airport and the plane that will fly me home. Only I'm not sure what home is anymore. It's been a thousand years since I dragged my things into this house, with Dad standing there furious, telling me I couldn't stay. What if I had left the next morning, like he wanted me to? Even now I don't know where I got the courage to defy him. How different my life would have been if I had left. No Thomas, no Erlita, or Lila or Ruth, and no paintings of mine hanging on the Tergiversate walls. A whole chunk of my life never lived. The worst thing that can happen isn't failing; it's not trying.

I ask Anita if she'll feed the cat. "That's a nasty cat," she says. "I don't know why you want it around." But she promises.

I go to say good-bye to Dad. We love each other,

but it's angry love. I resent his caring about his work more than he cared about me, but I have to take what I can get, and I guess it's better than nothing.

Dad is propped up in bed. "Get out," he says to Anita. "I want to talk to my daughter." Anita and I exchange a knowing look, and she stalks out of the studio.

"You think I'm selfish," Dad says.

"I don't know what to think about you," I say. "It'll probably take me the rest of my life to figure you out."

"I hope you'll have better things to think about. Like your painting."

"You said it was no good."

"I lied."

"Why?"

"Because I didn't want my daughter competing with me. Because I wanted to spare you the heartbreak I've had, and any good artist has, of always falling short of what you want to accomplish. The better you are, the higher the expectation gets. You never win."

"But it's not a game," I say. "It's just what you have to do."

All this talking is hard for Dad. He begins to cough, a choking cough that scares me. I call Anita, who reaches for the oxygen mask at Dad's bedside. He gulps air. Looking out the window, I see the taxi pull up. I take Dad's hand. His fingers close over mine. "Let me stay," I beg.

He shakes his head and gives me one of his wicked smiles.

Anita says, "Time to go."

Dad pulls away the mask. "Kate Quinn," he whispers. "Be Kate Quinn."

13

When I get home, Mom throws her arms around me like I've survived some scary life-threatening catastrophe. I guess I have. Of course she is devastated when I tell her I haven't been going to school. She's furious with Dad and doesn't want to hear a word about him. The only argument we have is when I tell her I'm changing my name to Kate Quinn.

"It's not fair," she says. "All these years he never gave you a thought." When that doesn't make me change my mind, she warns, "People will think you're trading on his name."

"I can't help what other people think. Anyhow, there aren't going to be any more paintings of Dad's. He wants to think of more paintings with the name Quinn on them. You're my mom and I love you, but you've got me; he's got nothing."

The next day I begin to ease back into my old life. I get up and look for something to have for breakfast, keeping quiet so I don't wake up Mom. This morning I find some croissants she's brought home from the restaurant and I have one with my coffee. There was a fog last night, and this morning when the sun comes out, I see that the drops of moisture on the branches have frozen into a thousand crystals of ice, glistening like shiny knives in the sun. I pull on my jacket and boots and head outside with the shovel to clear a path to Mom's car. I get the broom and sweep the light snow from the car's roof. Everything glitters and glistens. The most amazing thing is the silence. There is no silence like this in the city, only a constant background of hum and roar that leaks into your life and smothers your thoughts. I'm more sure than ever that when I finish school, this is where I'll settle down. You don't have to go to New York to be an artist. You need to paint where your heart is.

Dad died the day after his show opened. The Detroit papers had articles about "the famous recluse." The *New York Times* had a long obituary. Mom's name was there, and she hated it. So was mine. It called me Kate Quinn and said I was an aspiring artist. The obituary talked about how Dad had dropped out of the art scene and about his drinking problem. But most of the article was about the new show, with quotes from museum curators. The *New York Times*'s own art critic wrote of how brilliantly Dad's work illustrated the emptiness of a world where cars and houses and computers take the place of relationships with people.

There is one exception in all the article's praise. The writer says, "Some critics attack the ugliness and the anger in the paintings; other critics say that is

Quinn's strength. Quinn is not simply critical of what the world has become, but his paintings suggest he doesn't know what he would put in its place."

Morgan has kept in touch. The show has sold out, except for a couple of paintings Morgan is keeping for himself. He says they're an investment, because with no more Dalton Quinn paintings, the prices are sure to go up.

We learn from Mr. Krull that Dad wanted to be buried here in Larch. Mom and I are both shocked. "He won't leave us alone," Mom says. My guess is he didn't want a celebrity funeral with photographers and gossip. Or was he saying, "I'm finally coming back," and asking Mom and me to forgive him? Or maybe there was just no place else to go. I don't know.

At first Mom says she won't go to the funeral. "Why should I? I haven't seen him in years. He doesn't mean anything to me, and look how he used you."

"He didn't use me," I tell her. "I stayed because I wanted to." I can't help adding, "If you don't feel anything for Dad after all these years, why are you still so bitter?"

Mom gives me an angry look and goes into the tiny cubbyhole that is her bedroom, slamming the door after her. Trailer doors are too flimsy to really slam, but I get the idea. An hour later when she comes out, she says, "Maybe you're right—maybe it's time for me to let go. Anyhow, I don't want you to have to go to the funeral alone."

We go to our church together to explain to the pastor the complicated relationships among Dad and Mom and me, but Pastor Hoyer says of course he'll do the funeral. Anything for Mom, who has been active in the church. So it's Mom who gets Dad his funeral. "I hope Dalton appreciates it," Mom says with a rueful smile. It's the first time that Mom has ever accompanied Dad's name with a smile, even a skimpy one.

It's a small affair, just me and Mom and Mrs. Smouse, who goes to all the funerals at the church as a kind of entertainment, and some friends of Mom's from the resort and her bridge group. There are a few curious townspeople too. Mr. Krull comes up from Detroit, and there's a local reporter from the *Larch*

Chronicle. The surprising thing is that Morgan flies in. It's amazing meeting him in person after all the hundreds of calls and emails. He isn't at all like I pictured. He's short, with a shaved head and sad eyes, and he's dressed in New York City black: black turtleneck, black blazer, and black trench coat. New Yorkers are always ready for a funeral. After an awkward expression of sympathy Morgan looks around at the modest church and sprinkling of mourners.

"We could have given Dalton a terrific send-off," he says. "The papers would have covered it." He keeps looking around as if he can't believe Dad came from so small a town, as if a mistake has been made or something is being hidden from him. Finally he goes over to the reporter from the *Larch Chronicle* and starts to give her a lecture on Dad's painting in relation to contemporary art. She is startled and then a little desperate to get away from him, but Morgan isn't going to miss an opportunity.

The pastor has never met Dad and only knows he was once married to Mom and that he grew up here.

In his remarks the pastor quotes a passage from the Bible: "Where my treasure is, there will my heart be also." He says how the places where we grew up and the people we love stay with us all our lives. I thought about how Dad had run from Larch and about how much he left behind.

Immediately after the service Morgan takes off in a hired limousine for the airport in Traverse City. His last words as he makes his getaway: "Dalton must have seen something here I don't."

Mr. Krull asks to go back to our home with us. He seems surprised to find home is a trailer. Mom makes coffee for him. We want to be hospitable, and we appreciate his coming up for the service, but we really just want to be alone to deal with our feelings: my saying good-bye to Dad and Mom trying to figure out if there's a little bit of Dad she can forgive.

Mr. Krull sips his coffee, refusing the store-bought cookies I offer. He looks around doubtfully and says, "I don't suppose you'll be unhappy to find something a little more spacious."

In a frosty voice Mom says, "I don't know what you mean. We've been very happy here."

"Yes, yes, of course. It's very cozy." He reaches for his briefcase and reads Dad's will like he's a CEO giving a report to his board of directors. There's a lot of money from the sale of Dad's paintings. The show was a great success. Dad has left most of his money to the art school in Detroit for scholarships for students, but he's also left me money, enough to buy Mom a house and to put myself through school. Mr. Krull will be my trustee until I'm twenty-one to see that I don't blow it all on a trip around the world.

Before I can say anything, Mom says, "I've never taken a cent from Dalton and I won't now."

In a quiet voice Mr. Krull corrects her. "I understand how you feel, but he didn't leave it to you. He left it to Kate. It's for her to decide."

Mom stares at me. "He's a little late in considering you. I don't think you should accept his money."

I see Mom isn't going to forgive Dad after all. I think of how much of her life has been spent on this grudge, and it breaks my heart. But that's how she feels, not how I feel. I don't want to be disloyal, but I do want to make up my own mind. I say, "I want to go back to school, Mom."

"We'll find a way. We don't need his money. I'm making enough."

"Mom, I'm going to use what Dad left me. I don't want to be a part of your fight with Dad. I'm not taking sides. Just because I accept something from Dad doesn't mean I love you less."

"Take it if you want to, but I'm not going to move into a house paid for with Dalton's money. It's too late for him to make amends."

Mr. Krull looks at her and says in a quiet voice, "I often think the most generous person is the one receiving, not the one bestowing the gift."

Mom looks like someone hit her.

I sign papers and have things explained to me. Mr. Krull gives me his card with his office phone, his cell, his fax, and his email. Evidently we're going to have a lot of things to talk about. He shakes our hands politely and climbs back into his car, a modest black number, and backs slowly out of the driveway; although a car or two an hour on this road is the max, he looks carefully both ways. I'm sure my money will be well cared for and suspect he'll keep it under his mattress.

The next week Justin comes down from the Upper Peninsula for semester break. He tells me about his life up there in that north country, how they make the best of all the cold and snow by having a lot of festivals. They have dog races and ice-sculpture contests. He goes ice fishing and cross-country skiing. He loves school. He's entered some sort of math competition among university students across the country, and he's representing his college.

Finally he gets around to saying how sorry he is about Dad. He asks what I'm going to do now, but from his slightly abstracted look I suspect that all the while we talk, the bigger part of his brain is working on the math competition. When I mention the amount of money I'll have, he tells me how much I would earn each year if I invest it in bonds or the stock market or something called certificates of deposit. Once he hears about the money, he seems more interested in me. Not because I have it, but because even a small sum has so many mathematical possibilities.

Justin is Justin, a good friend, but nothing more. I think about Adam. There has to be someone out there for me, and I tell myself I have lots of time.

Dad's car was on its last legs, so I splurge for a decent used car that I can drive back and forth from school. Mom doesn't object; she's thinking I'll be able to come home more often. I find having your own car is like a passport to the world. Even if you never go farther than the end of the block, you know you *can* go all the way across the country if you want to.

On a mild February day, when the snow has melted into puddles, I head for Detroit. I've sent the school a CD with my most recent work and I've been accepted for the spring term. It's Valentine's Day and the students have created these amazing valentines. They're stuck up all over the school, so the first things I see when I walk into the building are hundreds of hearts. It's like they're saying, *Welcome back*. In the admitting office the counselor is friendly. "We'll be able to give you the same scholarship you had. Luckily we've had an endowment from a very famous artist, Dalton Quinn." She looks down at my application and smiles. "You share his last name. How appropriate."

I smile and say I won't need a scholarship, that like the school I was lucky enough to come into some money.

"Why how nice for you. A grandparent?"

"No, my father."

"Oh, I'm so sorry. He must have been very young to die."

"Yes," I say, and hurry out of her office before she puts it all together. I will have to learn to deal with people who do make the connection. It will be an advantage and a curse. People will be interested in my work because I am Dalton Quinn's daughter, but people will compare my work with my father's, and my work will suffer in comparison. At least our painting styles are very different. No one will be able to say I copied my father's style.

I have a room in the student dormitory now. The dorm was once an elegant apartment building, and along with the regulation utilitarian furniture there are graceful archways and high ceilings. From my window I see the Art Institute, where I can go to see Dad's painting anytime. After his show's success they moved it to a more prominent place.

I haven't seen Thomas, but there are stories in the newspaper every day of the trouble in Lebanon, and I imagine Thomas's and Mary's aunts and uncles and their children getting into airplanes and heading here, leaving the violence behind.

Sometimes I help out at Lila's. I did a mural of Belle Isle for one wall of the shop, and her designs look perfect hanging against the background of trees and water.

In the city, spring catches me unawares. One day there's gray, slushy snow on the streets and sidewalks, and the next day I see the blooms of forsythia and crocuses poking up. The banks along the expressways are greening up. At school some of our classes are held outdoors in the sculpture garden. At night when we head out of the dorm to get pizza, we make a point of leaving our jackets off, pretending it's summer.

I know spring in the city is hardly anything compared to what's happening up north. The alder bushes along the stream are in blossom, and in the woods the spring beauties and trout lilies and Dutchman's-breeches are spread out like a tapestry on the forest floor. On the lakes the migrating ducks have settled in, the buffleheads and mergansers and wood ducks with their clown faces. You have to be out nearly every second not to miss what's coming next. It kills me not to be there, not to paint it, because next spring everything will be a little different. I think of one of my favorite paintings. It's by Winslow Homer. It's summer. There's an open field of grass, probably a pasture, with a scattering of wildflowers. In the distance are trees and green hills. Some little boys, barefoot and wearing caps, are playing crack the whip. Homer makes you feel what it's like to be happy and free on a warm summer day. That's what I want to do. I want to make people feel what it's like to be in the woods, in the places where there are wildflowers but also in the dark places where hawks and foxes hunt.

One evening I drive by Dad's house. It's been sold, and I see a young couple sitting on the porch enjoying the warm evening. My memories of Dad come flooding back. I pull up a few blocks away and stop the car until I can pull myself together.

At school we've just hung the annual student exhibition. I can guess by looking at the paintings that a lot of my classmates paint what the fashionable artists are painting in New York. What's hot. There are students who try to shock the viewer like five-year-olds who get into mischief just for the attention. I see paintings that imitate my dad's work too. When I look at my own painting in the exhibition, I have to be honest and admit that there are paintings by other students that are a lot better than mine. I know how much I have to learn.

Of course I dream about being a famous artist like Dad, with my paintings in a New York gallery and hanging in a museum. I don't think that's going to happen. But here's what *is* going to happen: When I finish school, I'll go back home and I won't stop painting until everyone sees what I see, until they can look at my paintings and know the woods in the way I know them, with the different times of day and the different seasons. That's what paintings do—they add something to other people's lives. So I'll go on sharing my world, surprising myself. "Keep painting," Dad said. I will—and not just for me but for him too. I'll paint all the pictures he never got to paint, but they'll be mine.